*The Happy Hollisters
and the
Sea Turtle Mystery*

The Happy Hollisters and the Sea Turtle Mystery

BY JERRY WEST

Illustrated by Helen S. Hamilton

DOUBLEDAY & COMPANY, INC.
GARDEN CITY, NEW YORK
1964

FOREWORD

The idea for this story came to the author when he visited the west coast of Florida and the islands of Sanibel and Captiva. However, Santabella and Captive Islands in this book are make-believe and the characters are fictional.

Jerry West

Contents

*The Happy Hollisters
and the
Sea Turtle Mystery*

CHAPTER 1

CHARLIE TIGER TAIL

"Ninety—ninety-five—a hundred!" shouted Ricky Hollister, as he leaned against a tree with his eyes tightly shut. "Ready or not, here I come!"

The seven-year-old boy whirled about in the game of hide-and-seek. But there was no one on the broad green lawn surrounding the Hollister home on Pine Lake. Red-haired Ricky tiptoed to the hedge and parted it. Nobody!

A giggle sounded. The boy spun around and his gaze was caught by an odd-looking craft far out on the lake. He stared in amazement, then called out, "Yikes! Look at that funny boat!"

Silence. The hiding youngsters did not make a peep.

"I'm not fooling!" Ricky pleaded, keeping his eyes on the strange boat. "You all can come in home free. Honest. This isn't a trick!"

Out of the leafy tree dropped six-year-old Holly, her pigtails flying. Pam, ten, stepped from behind the garage. She had a sunny smile and fluffy golden hair. Pete's crew-cut head popped up behind a big azalea bush, and next to it an upside-down bushel basket flipped over. There was little dark-haired Sue. "Where's the funny boat?" she demanded.

"There! It's heading for our dock."

Pete, a handsome boy of twelve, raced ahead of the others to the shore front. They all stood on the wooden pier and watched the speeding boat.

The Hollisters had never seen one like it before. It was a wide flat-bottomed craft about twelve feet long. Up front were two seats, one back of the other. Higher up behind these was a single chair made of metal tubing, and sitting there was a bronze-skinned man with his left hand on a rudder stick. This moved two fins, like the tail end of an airplane, and between them was mounted a metal tube about three feet long.

"Crickets!" Pete called out as the boat whizzed past with a peculiar whistling sound. "That's a little jet motor."

"I've read about Florida air boats," Pam said. "Could this be one?"

The strange craft made a wide circle, skimming over the calm surface of Pine Lake. As it headed toward the shore again, a dark-haired boy of Pete's age ran into the yard.

"Hi, Dave!" Pete called. "Did you see that queer boat?"

"I thought maybe it was something your dad made," said Dave Mead, who was Pete's best friend.

"We've never seen it before," Ricky replied.

12

Just then all the children gasped at once as the boat took a backward flip. The driver was thrown from his seat and hit the water with a splash. The craft sank beneath the surface!

For an instant the youngsters were stunned. Then Pete cried, "Come on, we must save him! Holly! Ricky! Go tell Mother!"

As Pete stepped down into their rowboat, he added, "Dave, I'll need your help, and yours, too, Pam." The two boys each took an oar, and rowed toward the place where the boat had sunk.

"There he is!" Pam called out as they neared the spot. Several yards ahead was a man, floating on his face.

"He must have been knocked out," Pete said as he pulled alongside the drifting figure. "Give me a hand, Dave."

The two boys tugged at the limp victim and pulled him over the gunwale into the bottom of the boat. Pete and Pam gave artificial respiration for a few minutes and the man's eyes blinked open.

"Who are you?" was Pete's first question.

The man uttered something which sounded like "Tiger Tail." Then he lapsed into unconsciousness.

"Jimminy!" Dave said. "Tiger Tail isn't any name. He must be delirious."

Pam rested the man's head against her arm, while Pete and Dave rowed toward shore as fast as they could. Halfway to the Hollisters' dock, a canoe with

"*Give me a hand, Dave.*"

two boys aboard glided past them. In it were Joey Brill and Will Wilson.

"We saw that boat, too!" cried Joey. He was a heavy-set boy about Pete's age, whose chief delight was bullying younger children. His dark-haired companion liked to do just what Joey did.

"We can claim it for our own," Will said, as he dug his paddle into the water.

"You'll do nothing of the sort!" Pam exclaimed. "The boat belongs to this poor man. He's hurt."

Ignoring Pam's good deed, Joey made a face at her and paddled toward the spot where the craft had sunk.

When the rowboat reached the dock, Mrs. Hollister and the other three children were waiting. Their mother was a pretty, slender woman with blond hair. Her face, usually smiling, was full of anxiety as she helped Pete and Dave lift the injured man onto the dock.

"Let's put him in this lawn chair," Mrs. Hollister directed the two boys.

"I've already telephoned to Officer Cal," Ricky said. "He's bringing the Emergency Squad."

No sooner had he spoken than the wailing siren could be heard far down the road. The emergency truck roared into the Hollisters' driveway, halted, and three men ran to the dock. One of them was Cal Newberry, a pleasant-faced young officer who had worked with the Hollister children on some of the mysteries they had solved.

The first-aid men examined the dripping-wet boatman. "No broken bones," Officer Cal said, smiling.

The man's eyes opened again and he looked about, bewildered. "Where am I?"

"You're all right," Officer Cal assured him. "What is your name?"

"Charlie Tiger Tail," the man said, sitting up and rubbing his head. "I had an accident."

"You hit the water awfully hard," Pam said sympathetically.

"Is that your real name?" Ricky asked. "I don't know anybody else named Tiger Tail."

The man's bronze face lighted up in a smile. "That's because there aren't any Seminole Indians around Shoreham," he said.

"You are a Seminole?" asked Mrs. Hollister.

"Yes," he said, then stopped abruptly and pointed out on the lake. "Are those two boys trying to get my boat?"

Joey Brill was leaning over the end of the canoe, reaching down into the water.

"Get away from there, Joey!" Pete called.

"It's our boat and we're going to keep it!" Will bellowed.

"Oh, no you're not," shouted Officer Cal. He hurried to the Hollisters' boat and stepped into it. Instantly Joey and Will sped off.

"I'll get you for telling the cops, Pete Hollister!" Joey yelled, shaking his fist.

When they had disappeared around the bend, Officer Cal got back on the dock. "I'll notify the Pine Lake Patrol," he said. "We'll get your boat for you, Mr. Tiger Tail."

"But now you'd better change those wet things," said Pam. She and her mother led the Indian into the house where Mrs. Hollister gave him towels and dry clothes.

Meanwhile the other children followed the policeman to the truck radio and watched while he sent a message to headquarters. Then he and his two rescue buddies drove off.

"I have to go on an errand," Dave said. "So long."

When Charlie Tiger Tail reappeared in the backyard with Pam and her mother, he was wearing one of Mr. Hollister's sport shirts and a fresh pair of khaki trousers. They had been rolled up at the bottom, for the Indian, although sturdily built, was shorter than the children's father.

Charlie Tiger Tail told them that he was a guide who took people on air-boat trips in the Florida Everglades. "I have two boats," he said, "but brought only one to Shoreham on an auto-trailer. This craft used to be driven by an airplane propeller. However, I wanted to have the fastest one in the Everglades."

"So you came to the jet factory in Shoreham!" Pete guessed.

"That's right," the Seminole went on. He explained that he had purchased a small jet engine, and had mounted it on his craft. "But it doesn't balance too well, I'm afraid," he said.

"Oh, don't worry. Daddy will help you fix it," Ricky declared.

"Why do you have to have the fastest boat in the Neverglades?" little Sue chirped.

"Everglades, silly," Holly said, pinching her sister's pink cheek. "That's a place in Florida."

"I'm a deputy sheriff," the Indian replied, "and I have to catch turtle poachers. They have fast boats, so mine must be faster."

Before the youngsters could ask more questions, the patrol launch hove into sight. As it came alongside the Hollisters' dock, Pete and Ricky both greeted the three policemen on it and jumped aboard.

"You take it easy, Mr. Tiger Tail," Pete called back, "and we'll help find your air boat."

The boys and the police headed toward the spot where the odd craft had disappeared.

"It's right about here," Pete said.

The police launch stopped and the men lowered a grappling hook on the end of a long rope. They dragged it back and forth over the lake bottom.

"There, we've got something!" one of the policemen exclaimed.

With Pete's help the three men pulled on the rope. The hook had caught on the seat framework, and soon the air boat emerged from the water.

The launch's motor started again, and the Florida craft was eased toward the Hollisters' dock. There the boys helped haul it onto the shore.

"It doesn't look as if any damage was done," Pete remarked, as they thanked the policemen.

"Glad to help you," the officer in charge said, and gave a crisp salute.

As the patrol boat left, a station wagon pulled into the driveway. Out stepped Mr. Hollister, a tall, athletic-looking man. He strode briskly down to the group at the dock.

"Pam telephoned me," he said. "I understand we have a visitor from Florida."

Charlie Tiger Tail shook hands with Mr. Hollister. "I'm sorry to cause you so much trouble," he said.

"None at all," his host replied, smiling. "So this is your air boat. Quite a contraption! Your jet unit is located too far back, though. I think that's what made you flip over."

"I'm not an engineer," the Seminole said.

"I think we can fix the trouble," Mr. Hollister assured him. "Why don't you be our guest? We'll take your boat to my workshop behind The Trading Post." This was Mr. Hollister's sporting goods, hardware, and toy store in the center of Shoreham.

"Oh, no thank you," the Indian said shyly. "You see, I'm staying at a motel down—"

"We'd be glad to have you visit us," the children's mother said with a friendly smile.

19

"And you can tell us about the Seminole Indians," Holly put in.

"Are poachers bad men?" Ricky spoke up.

"Oh yes. They kill the giant sea turtles, and that's illegal," the Seminole replied. "They also steal the turtles' eggs. When I promised the police to help catch these poachers they made me a deputy."

"That is why he wants a real fast boat, Dad," Ricky said.

"And there is another reason, too," Charlie Tiger Tail said slowly in a serious voice. "I may need it when I investigate Captive Island. That's near where I live. Something mysterious is going on out there."

"Oh, please tell us about it!" Pam said.

"It might be too spooky," Charlie Tiger Tail replied, shaking his head.

CHAPTER 2

A MISSING GIFT

"Your mystery wouldn't be too scary for us!" Holly declared, her eyes dancing.

"We're detectives," Ricky told the Seminole proudly.

"But this is such a weird case, perhaps no one can solve it," the Indian replied. "All right, I'll stay with you while my boat is being repaired, because Holly reminds me of my own little girl."

"You have a daughter?" Pam asked.

"Yes, her name is Clementine and she is ten years old." Charlie Tiger Tail explained that Clementine was staying with her grandmother in a Seminole Indian village until he returned.

"Hop into my station wagon," Mr. Hollister said. "We'll go to your motel and get your things."

In less than half an hour the men returned. Following the Hollisters' car was a half-ton pickup truck with a trailer hitch and a boat carrier. Charlie Tiger Tail parked beside their garage, and got out with a suitcase in one hand. In the other, he held two small boxes.

"Here are gifts for you children," he said. "This one is for the girls and the other for the boys."

Pam opened the box he gave her and peered inside. "Oh, beautiful sea shells!" she exclaimed.

"They're keen!" declared Holly.

Charlie Tiger Tail said the shells had come from Santabella Island. He had gathered them to give to some Seminole children, but had not had the opportunity to deliver the shells. "I can get them more," he added.

"And what are these?" Pete asked, opening the boys' gift.

"They're called ligs."

"What?" asked Ricky.

"Tree snails." Their visitor explained that the creatures were common in southwest Florida. As the boys looked at the red- and yellow-banded shell in Pete's palm, it began to move.

"Yikes, it's alive!" Ricky exclaimed.

"Shall we put them on trees?" Pete asked.

When the Indian nodded, the boys took the half-dozen ligs, ran over to a small tree beside the lake, and attached the snails to the smooth bark.

"See how they glisten in the sunshine!" Pam remarked as she admired the beautiful creatures. Just then Zip, the Hollisters' collie dog, bounded across the lawn to the tree. He stopped short and barked, his nose close to the snails.

"Don't hurt them!" cried Holly.

Zip sniffed at the colorful shells, and his tail began to wag.

"They're friends already," Pam said, laughing. "Now Zip, meet Mr. Tiger Tail."

The Seminole's dark eyes gleamed with pleasure as he stroked the collie's long thick fur. Presently Mr. Hollister reminded them that it was almost time for dinner. With Ricky racing ahead, they trooped into the house.

As they waited to be called to the table, Pam and Holly sat on the sofa beside Charlie Tiger Tail, and the Indian named the sea shells.

"This is a Rose Murex," he said, picking out a small pink one. "And a Tulip," he went on, showing them a fat one with pointed ends. "This shiny one is a Jewel Box, and these are Angel Wings."

"They're beautiful," Pam said. "What's this one with a design like Chinese writing?"

"It's a Chinese Alphabet Cone," the Seminole replied, and added, "I wish I had a Lion's Paw."

"A real lion's paw?" asked Ricky, seated cross-legged on the rug.

"No, it's a rare shell which resembles one."

At the dinner table, their guest told something about the Indians in his area. The original tribe was called the Calusas, but they had died out many years before.

"Were they fierce, Mr. Tiger Tail?" Ricky asked.

"Sometimes," the man replied. "In fact, it was a Calusa arrow which fatally wounded Ponce de

León, the Spanish explorer." Then he added with a big smile, "Why don't you all just call me Charlie?"

"Even me?" asked Sue. When the Indian nodded, she said, "Okay, Charlie."

The Seminole Indians, Charlie continued, were remnants of several tribes driven from north Florida and Georgia. They never surrendered to the Spanish or the Americans. "Officially we have never signed a treaty," he said, then added with a wink, "but we're peaceful Indians now."

After breakfast next morning Pete and Ricky hurried down to the tree by the shore front. There were the snails, still clinging to the bark only a few inches from where they had been left the day before.

The boys helped their father and Charlie drag the air boat onto the trailer, which bore a license plate reading: SEMINOLE INDIAN.

"Yikes! That's keen!" Ricky said. "I wish we could have a license like that."

When the two men drove off to The Trading Post, the boys returned to the lake front to look at the snails again. They had vanished!

"Look!" Ricky cried. "I know where our ligs went!" He pointed offshore, where Joey and Will were paddling away in a canoe.

"Stop!" Pete yelled. "Give us back our snails!"

Joey looked over his shoulder and made a face.

"You think you're smart because an Indian is staying with you!" he called.

"We're going to cook the snails and eat them," Will taunted.

"You'd better not!" Pete warned. But Joey and Will paddled fast and soon disappeared from sight.

Pete and Ricky trudged into the house to find their sisters seated around a card table in the living room playing with the shells. Pam was reading aloud from the encyclopedia. "I found out some more about the Everglades," she said.

Pam explained that the region was not all a thick swamp of trees, moss, and vines. Much of the area was open grassy marsh lying in clear shallow water. "It flows from Lake Okeechobee to the Gulf of Mexico," she said, tracing her finger over an illustrated map. "And it's full of wild animals—black bears, otters, snakes, alligators, and crocodiles.

"And the alligators and crocodiles are protected by the law from poachers, too," she said, "same as the sea turtles."

"Come on, Pete," Ricky urged. "We'd better hurry if we want to get our snails back."

The brothers hastened out, hopped on their bicycles and pedaled to Joey's house. But no one answered the doorbell, and neither the bully nor his friend Will could be seen anywhere about.

On the way home Ricky said, "I think Dad could sell some of those shells at The Trading Post. We could all go to Florida to get them ourselves."

Pete grinned. "We can dream, can't we?"

The snail snitchers kept out of sight, though

Ricky and Pete looked for them until midafternoon. It was then they heard the station-wagon horn and dashed out to meet their father. Charlie drove behind with his trailer, and on it was the jet air boat.

"Now I think the motor's placed right," Mr. Hollister said, as he gave Ricky an affectionate pat.

"When're you going to try it out?" Pete asked.

"Tonight, after supper," his father replied. They helped Charlie detach the trailer hitch and pull the two-wheel vehicle to the water's edge.

"Now," said Pete, "she's all set to go. I wish we could help you catch the turtle poachers in this."

After dinner, Pam found their guest alone in the living room.

"Charlie," she said, "there's something I just have to ask you."

"What is that?"

"The real spooky mystery—what is it?"

Before he could answer, Ricky appeared in the doorway. "Come on, Charlie! Everybody's ready to test the boat!"

"I'll tell you later," the Seminole promised Pam. They hurried down to the dock where the others were waiting.

The boys helped slide the air boat into the lake. Then the Indian climbed in and sat on the high seat. Mr. Hollister took his place in the front. The Indian pressed a button. After a small whirring sound, the jet motor came to life in a thin whistling sound.

"Stand back," the Seminole said, "so I can give it more power."

The children scampered halfway to the house. Charlie pressed the accelerator with his right foot. The jet whistled louder and the boat headed out into the lake.

"She sure is a beaut!" Pete exclaimed, as the Everglades craft gathered speed. It flashed around in a wide circle, then headed in toward the sloping sandy patch on the shore beside the dock. Nearby, under a large willow tree lay the Hollisters' cat, White Nose, with her five kittens. On and on came the boat.

"It's going to hit the shore!" Pam cried out.

But Charlie Tiger Tail did not seem concerned. He aimed the craft directly for the sandy spot. It roared onto the shore and right across the lawn. White Nose and her family scampered up a tree before the boat came to rest beside the Hollisters' home.

"Yikes, that was super!" Ricky exclaimed and did two cart wheels as he approached the air boat.

"A real thrill!" Mr. Hollister said, as he stepped out.

"Now you see how we go in shallow water—or no water at all?" Charlie asked with a chuckle.

The boys helped to drag the boat back into the lake.

"May we have a ride, too?" Holly asked.

The air boat roared onto the shore.

"Sure. Now that my boat is safe, we can take the whole family," their guest replied.

"But not up onto the lawn for me!" Mrs. Hollister pleaded laughingly.

She stepped into the boat and held Sue on her lap. Beside her sat Pam. Directly behind, Pete, Ricky, and Holly took their places.

The motor started again and Charlie guided the craft out across Pine Lake, with Zip, the collie, barking loudly from the shore.

As the air boat scooted back and forth, some people watching at the water's edge waved their handkerchiefs, and the Hollisters waved back. But the onlooker they did not expect to see when they arrived at their dock was Joey Brill! He stood there with Will at his side.

"What are you doing here?" Pete asked.

"We want our ligs," Ricky said.

"Don't worry," Joey replied, managing a half smile. "We were only borrowing them."

"We'd like a ride on that thing," Will said.

"Are these the boys who tried to get my boat when it was sunk?" Charlie Tiger Tail asked.

"It was only a joke," Joey said. "We'll return the snails, too, if you give us a ride."

Charlie looked doubtfully at Mr. Hollister, and when he nodded yes, the Indian said, "Well, jump in and I'll take you."

Joey and Will sat on the front seat, and the air boat started off again. But they had not gone far before Joey stood up and raised his arms like airplane wings.

"Oh dear!" Pam said. "He doesn't know the first rule of boating."

The air boat made one circle, then came back. As Joey and Will stepped off, the Indian pursed his lips and shook his head. Without a word, Joey and Will dashed for their bicycles parked in front of the house and pedaled off.

"Thank you, John, for fixing my air boat," Charlie Tiger Tail said, shaking Mr. Hollister's hand. "She works perfectly now, so I can leave for Florida."

"And catch the turtle poachers," said Pete.

"But not before you tell us about the other mystery," Pam reminded him.

As dusk began to settle over Pine Lake, the Seminole sat on the grass with the children surrounding him.

"I have a chickee on Turtle Point near the Thousand Islands and the Everglades."

"Only one chicken?" Sue piped up.

The Indian threw back his head and laughed. "A chickee," he said, "is a Seminole Indian house." He told them it was constructed of poles and a thatched roof. "But the sides are open," he added.

"Let him tell the mystery," Holly said impatiently.

"Just offshore from where I live," the Indian said, "are two small islands, named Santabella and

Captive. At low tide you can walk from one to the other. Now, *this* mystery—" He paused and looked doubtfully around at their eager faces.

"Please go on," Pam pleaded.

"There is an eerie sound which comes from Captive Island. It is heard only at night."

"Could it be made by an animal?" Pete asked.

"No," said Charlie firmly. "I know the calls of all the animals in the Everglades. Never have I heard anything like this.

"People used to visit the island and look for shells," he added, "but the strange sound has frightened everyone away."

"I wish we could go to Florida and solve the mystery," Pete said.

"At the same time we could get shells to sell at The Trading Post, Dad," Ricky put in.

"That's a fine idea," Charlie said with a wide grin. "Then you could come and live in my chickee. It's primitive and rather wild."

"Oh, that would be just neat!" Holly exclaimed.

"Would you do it?" the Seminole asked, looking at the children's parents.

"We could stand a vacation about now, John," Mrs. Hollister said smilingly.

The Seminole suggested that the family stay at the Pelican Beach Hotel, about thirty miles north of his place. "I can pick you up there and take you to my chickee," he offered.

"Let's go then," Mr. Hollister said.

The children leaped to hug him with such force that he was nearly borne to the ground.

"Oh, Daddy, you're wonderful! I love you!" Holly said, as she squeezed him hard.

So it was agreed they would meet Tiger Tail in one week at Pelican Beach. At that moment Joey Brill pedaled his bike into the drive. It was nearly dark and he had his headlight on.

"We're going to Florida!" little Sue blurted out.

"Oh, don't tell him," Pam whispered, but it was too late.

"That's nothing! I'm going to Florida too," Joey replied.

"When?" Pete asked, walking up to him.

"In about a week," the bully said. "We've been there for vacations lots of times."

Was he telling the truth, Pete wondered, or only bragging?

"Here're your old ligs," Joey said, thrusting out a brown paper sack.

Pete took it and reached inside.

"Ouch!" he cried, jerking his hand out.

CHAPTER 3

THE MYSTERIOUS SPEAR

As JOEY Brill fled, Pete dropped the bag. A small snapping turtle clung to his middle finger. The next minute the little creature dropped onto the grass.

"What a mean trick to play!" Pam exclaimed.

Ricky picked up the frightened turtle and ran down to the dock to put it into the water. Meanwhile Pete peered cautiously into the brown bag. All of the ligs were there.

"Well, at least we've got our snails back safely," he said, as they went into the house.

Mrs. Hollister examined his finger, and found only a small scratch to which she applied antiseptic.

"It's good you weren't bitten by a giant sea turtle," Charlie told Pete. "Wait until you see them! They're so big a child can ride on their backs!"

Later that evening Mr. Hollister telephoned the hotel at Pelican Beach and made reservations. He told the manager the family would arrive in four days.

"We will fly down and rent a car when we get there," Mr. Hollister said.

Early next morning the air boat was mounted on

the trailer, and the Hollisters said good-by to their new friend.

"I'll meet you in a week," Charlie told them, "and you can go to work on both mysteries. Unless," he added with a wink, "I've caught the turtle poachers by then."

"Oh, don't do that!" Ricky exclaimed. "We want to help you!"

"Don't worry," the Indian assured him. "Even with the faster boat, it won't be so easy."

Waving good-bys, Charlie pulled his trailer into the street and soon was out of sight.

"We ought to take a gift to Clementine," Pam said as they went into the house.

"How about a doll from The Trading Post, Daddy?" Holly asked.

"All right," her father agreed. "You girls come down this morning and pick one out."

"Oh wonderful!" Pam said. "And we'll make an extra outfit for it, too!"

Within an hour they had brought home a pretty blond bride doll and were busily cutting out a blue dress and hat for her.

Excitement gripped all the Hollisters. Everyone was busy making preparations to visit the Everglades.

On Saturday, Pam and Holly helped their mother clean the house and between chores they worked on the blue outfit. When it was finished, they placed it with the new doll in Pam's suitcase.

After church on Sunday, Ricky glanced into Sue's room. "You're packing enough things to stay for a year!" he said. Cases lay open and clothes were spread neatly on the bed. Several old dolls were included as well as costume jewelry. Sue laid out a little gold bracelet which she took with her everywhere she went.

"Girls need lots of things," she declared, tilting up her chin. "Boys are different."

That afternoon the children left their pets with special friends who had promised to take care of them. Mr. Hollister had already made arrangements for his business to be run by the employees.

On the morning of their departure, Sue wore her gold bracelet. Mr. Hollister drove his family to the airport, and put the station wagon in the parking lot, where he would pick it up on their return.

The flight to the South was smooth and speedy. After the plane had landed at a big airport, Mr. Hollister rented a car. Soon they were skimming along the highway toward Pelican Beach.

"How flat and sandy Florida is!" said Holly.

Finally they drove into the hotel grounds. "Oh, what a beautiful place!" Pam exclaimed.

Before them stood a white building, three stories high. It faced on the Gulf of Mexico. The narrow beach had sparkling white sand, and along the high-water line lay a ruffle of sea shells.

Between the shore and the hotel were shuffle-board courts and a fresh-water swimming pool. Behind the building lay a broad golf course.

As soon as the family was shown its suite of rooms, the children hurried into their bathing suits and ran toward the beach.

"Oh, isn't the Gulf of Mexico blue!" Pam exclaimed, as she wet her toes in the frothy surf made by the tiny waves.

"Yikes, it's calm!" Ricky said and splashed out to swim.

"The water's warm," Sue said with a giggle as a ripple washed over her feet.

"Oh, Sue, you didn't take off your bracelet," Pam said. "Here, give it to me."

"I'll be careful of it," replied the little girl, pulling away. She walked up on the beach, fell to her knees, and scooped up sand to make a castle.

The youngsters splashed in and out of the surf, played in the sand, and gathered shells in plastic buckets, which the hotel provided for its guests.

Several other children and a few grownups were also enjoying the beach and the hot sun.

"Florida is such fun!" Ricky said.

"Don't forget we're here to solve a mystery," Pam reminded him.

"Right. We'll have to start working on it," Pete agreed. "We can't play all the time." He took another dive into the surf, and when he returned he heard Sue crying.

"What's the matter, honey?" he asked. "Did a giant sea turtle nip you?"

"Did a giant sea turtle nip you?"

"I lost my bracelet," she said.

"Maybe a fish made off with it," Ricky said, joking. But this made Sue cry even harder.

Just then a girl about fifteen, wearing a candy-striped bathing suit, passed by, looking for shells. "I know someone who might help you," she said. "Uncle Dan, the magic man."

"Is he a magician? And can he make things appear?" Pete asked doubtfully.

The girl told them that Uncle Dan was a retired fisherman who lived in a cottage not far down the beach. He had a metal detector. "Finding things is his hobby," she said, "and he'll be glad to help you."

The girl pointed out the cottage and Pete trotted along the sand toward it with Ricky and Holly at his heels. Pam remained behind with Sue.

When Pete neared the place he ran across the beach, took the wooden steps two at a time, then knocked on the door. A robust, elderly man with rosy cheeks answered.

"Are you Uncle Dan, the magic man?" Ricky asked him.

"That I am. Did you lose something?"

When Pete told about Sue's bracelet, Uncle Dan said, "I'll help you, but first come inside and see what I have here."

The children stepped into a living room, and on one side saw a long table. Lying upon it were scores of articles including pocketknives, jewelry, pens, buttons, cigarette lighters, and other trinkets made of metal.

"Yikes!" Ricky said. "You found all of these?"

"And do you sell them?" Pete asked.

Uncle Dan said no. He kept them sometimes for months until their owners came to claim them. "But some people never come," he said.

The children looked at the treasures, while Uncle Dan went into a back room. He reappeared carrying a long metal stick. Attached to one end of it was a round metal disk. A wire led from the stick to earphones which the man wore over his head.

"Come on now, we'll look for the bracelet," he said.

Holly skipped along the beach beside Uncle Dan, plying him with questions about his discoveries.

"Did you ever find pirates' gold, or cannons or anything like that?" she asked.

"Nothing that exciting," Uncle Dan said, as they approached Pam and Sue.

After Pete had made introductions, Uncle Dan quickly adjusted his earphones and moved the metal disk back and forth across the sand.

"How can you tell when you find something?" Pam wanted to know.

The man explained that the detector made a faint clicking sound in his ears. Whenever metal lay under the sand, the sound grew very loud.

"Oh-oh! Here's a noisy one," he said. "Dig in this spot, sonny!"

Ricky pawed the sand like a dog digging up a long-buried bone. Finally his fingers grasped the strap of a broken bathing cap. On the end was a metal clip.

"False alarm," Uncle Dan said, smiling, "but don't worry. We'll keep trying."

Back and forth he moved the detector, closer to the foaming water line. Finally he said, "Ouch, here's another loud one!"

This time Holly dug into the sand. Then she let out a yelp. "Here it is! I've found the bracelet!"

"It probably fell off your sister's arm and rolled down here to the water's edge," Uncle Dan guessed.

The children thanked the man for his kindness. As Uncle Dan started back toward his cottage, Holly trailed along beside him.

"Could I try using your detector once?" she asked in a small voice.

"Do you think a little girl like you can handle this?" he asked kindly.

"Oh, sure I can! See my muscle?" Holly said, flexing her arm.

"I guess you are pretty strong at that," came the reply as the man fitted the earphones over her head.

Holly picked up the detector with both hands. It was heavy for her, but she dragged it across the sand.

"I only hear little noises," she said, looking up at Uncle Dan. "Wait, there's a louder one." She put down the detector and began digging. There was a shiny dime.

"That wasn't lost too long ago," Uncle Dan said.

"May I keep it?"

"Of course. It's your treasure," he answered, laughing.

"Maybe I'll find a whole treasure chest," Holly declared. Delighted with her good luck, she dragged the detector back and forth, finally going to a high part of the beach between two scrubby cedar trees.

"You won't find anything up there," Uncle Dan called.

As he said this, Holly's eyes grew almost as wide as the detector itself. "I've found it! I've found the chest of gold!" she cried out.

The man hastened to her side. They started digging, and a moment later Holly's fingers found a round metal bar. Tugging with both hands, she freed it from the sand.

"It isn't a pirate's chest after all," she said in disappointment.

Uncle Dan gave a low whistle. "You've found something very important, young lady," he said. "This is a poacher's spear. We must report it to the police!"

CHAPTER 4

FOR BOYS ONLY

"RICKY! Pete! Pam!" Holly shouted excitedly, holding the long metal spear in her hands. "Hurry up! I found a clue!"

"Calm down, young lady," Uncle Dan said. "This is evidence that poachers have been here. The police might want it kept quiet."

The other children, hearing their sister's cry, came running along the beach. Holly told them what had happened and Uncle Dan explained the sharp-pointed metal shaft. He said that when turtles lay their eggs on the beach, they rough up a large area of sand with their flippers.

"So the exact spot where the nest is will not be easily detected. Is that right?" Pete asked.

"That's true," the man replied.

"But what does the spear have to do with it?" Ricky asked.

Uncle Dan said that poachers walk around the disturbed area, stabbing the weapon into the sand. "When the point comes up with yolk on it," he told them, "the thieves know that the nest is underneath."

"Oh dear," Pam said. "Then they dig down and steal the eggs!"

"That's mean!" piped up Sue.

"So the poor baby turtles never hatch out!" said Holly.

"No, they don't," Uncle Dan replied. "The eggs are sold."

"Are they good to eat?" Ricky asked.

"Yes, indeed," replied Uncle Dan. "In olden times some of the finest pastries in New Orleans were made with turtle eggs. In fact, the hunters took so many of them and killed the big turtles, too, that the creatures were almost wiped out. That's why the law protects them now."

Pete and Pam volunteered to carry the poacher's spear to headquarters, and Uncle Dan gave them directions.

The children hurried back to the beach, picked up their buckets of shells, and returned to the hotel, where they found their parents relaxing on a shady patio.

Proudly, Holly showed her find and told about it.

"You've made a flying start on your mystery," Mr. Hollister declared.

"But before you do any more sleuthing we'd better have lunch," their mother said. "Run along and dress."

Fifteen minutes later the family was enjoying sandwiches and frosty lemonade on the patio. When they had finished, Pete and Pam hurried to the golf-

43

caddy house where they had seen bicycles for rent. They quickly hired two. Pete placed the spear across his handle bars and the two children set off to the police station, which was located near the center of the small town.

The road led half a mile along the golf course before it intersected with the main street. As the children were about to make a right turn there, Pete heard an automobile coming up behind them. He pulled over to the side of the road, motioning with his left hand for the car to pass.

The vehicle, a black and white sedan, drew abreast of the boy, and forced him off the road. Surprised, Pete straddled his bike and looked at the car. The right front door opened and a man jumped out. He was short, heavily tanned, and wore a handkerchief tied around his forehead.

"Where did you get that spear?" he asked roughly.

"We found it on the beach," Pete replied, as Pam wheeled her bicycle up beside him.

"A friend of the poachers, eh?" the stranger asked unpleasantly.

"Of course not," Pam retorted. She tried to get a good look at the man in the driver's seat. But he was slouched low behind the steering wheel, and his straw hat was pulled down over his forehead.

"Give it to me," the short man demanded.

"But we're going to take it to the police station," Pete protested, moving away from the fellow.

"Give it to me!"

Without another word, the man grabbed the spear, at the same time giving Pete a shove. The boy fell down with his bike and the man sprang into the car, slamming the door.

"Wait, come back!" Pam cried out, but the automobile shot around the corner and was gone before Pete could get to his feet.

"Pam, did you get their license number?" he asked.

"Oh yes," she replied, "but I can't believe it. It's a Seminole Indian plate."

"I don't believe they're Seminole!" Pete said hotly. "Come on, let's go to the police."

Pedaling as fast as they could, the children rode to the small stucco station house and parked their bicycles. Entering, they walked over the cool terrazzo floor to a desk. Behind it sat a young man wearing a natty police uniform, open at the collar. He had straight brown hair, neatly combed, and keen gray eyes.

"I'm Sergeant Reno," he said. "May I help you?"

"Somebody stole a poacher's metal spear from us," Pete said.

The officer frowned. "What were you doing with it?"

Pete and Pam poured forth the story of Holly's find on the beach. Then Pam told of the Seminole Indian license plate.

"I know about that," Sergeant Reno said. "The

auto was reported stolen." Without a moment's hesitation he reached for his radio phone and broadcast the alarm to the patrol cars. "Thank you for being such good detectives," he said to the children.

"If you catch the men, will you let us know?" Pete asked. He then gave the sergeant their address, and he and Pam left the police station. But as they were about to pick up their bikes, they noticed a large yellow bus parked at one side of the building. Written on it in big black letters were the words: JUNIOR DEPUTY SHERIFFS.

"Junior Deputy Sheriffs!" Pete said. "I never heard of that before."

"Do you think it is something like our Detective Club in Shoreham?" Pam asked.

"Let's find out," her brother replied, and they hastened back inside.

Officer Reno told them that there were six hundred children from the fourth to the eighth grades organized as junior deputy sheriffs. "They learn the laws of the county, have picnics and ball games, and besides that," he continued with a smile, "they sometimes turn in tips to the police."

"Crickets! That's great," Pete said. "Do they—"

His question was interrupted by the buzz of the radio phone. The officer picked it up, smiled, and said, "Good work. Bring them in."

"Did they catch the men?" Pam asked.

The policeman shook his head. "They found the car," he said, "but the men made their getaway."

Pam looked puzzled. "But you just said—"

The sergeant interrupted with a smile. "The patrolmen did find something that might interest you. I'll keep it a secret until they return. By the way," the man added, "our junior deputies will be here to hold a meeting in a few minutes. Why don't you stay around?"

"Thanks! That'll be super," Pete said. He and Pam sat quietly on a bench for a while, then decided to wait outside. They stepped out of the door just in time to see the black and white sedan arrive.

As they ran to the curb, another young officer got out. He was a tall, thin-faced man. "My name's Hilton," he said. "Are you the children who gave us the tip?"

When Pete said yes, the policeman opened the back door, reached inside and emerged with an armful of crinkly hides.

"Alligator skins!" Pam cried out.

"That's the surprise," said Sergeant Reno, who had followed them out into the sunshine.

"Ample proof that the fugitives were poachers," he said. Officer Hilton explained that killing alligators for their hides was illegal in Florida.

"Many of our birds and beasts have had to be protected by law," he added, "or unscrupulous hunters would have killed them off."

"This car was stolen from an Indian camp down south near the Everglades," the sergeant said.

"Maybe these thieves were part of the poaching

gang that Charlie Tiger Tail is looking for," Pam suggested.

"Charlie Tiger Tail!" Officer Hilton exclaimed. "You know him?"

Pete grinned and said they did. But before he could tell his story about the jet air boat, a group of laughing boys ran down the street, shouting their greetings to the two policemen. They all wore shorts and white skivvy shirts with the words JUNIOR DEPUTY SHERIFF written across the front.

"They're keen!" Pete exclaimed.

"Pete, Pam," Officer Reno said, "I'd like you to meet some of our fellows. Here are three of the lieutenants, Bud Lardner, Alf Cohen, and Wyn Gillis." Bud was a tall, bony boy with freckles. Alf, who was slight with dark hair, gave a big friendly grin. Wyn was a sturdy towhead with a square jaw.

Pete shook hands with each one and Pam smiled shyly.

"I was telling Pete and Pam about our junior deputy sheriffs," the officer went on. "I think that Pete is a likely candidate. He just helped us locate a stolen car."

"Pam helped, too," said Pete.

"There aren't any girls in the deputy sheriffs," Bud explained, looking somewhat apologetic.

"There was one, remember?" Wyn put in. "We made her an honorary member because she rescued a kid in the Gulf."

49

"How about filling an application to join our bunch, Pete?" Alf invited.

"Could my brother Ricky be a member too?" the Hollister boy asked.

Receiving permission for this, he and Pam went inside and Pete made out two applications. Just as he handed them to Sergeant Reno, another uniformed man entered the station. He was introduced to the children as George Mark, a conservation officer.

"I heard that you found a poacher's spear," he addressed Pete and Pam. "Could you tell me exactly where?"

After Pete had given the location, Mr. Mark said that he would patrol the shore in his boat that night in case the poachers should return.

"Maybe we could help by keeping watch on the beach," Bud Lardner suggested. "Will you come with us, Pete?"

"Sure. When?"

It was decided that Bud, Alf, and Wyn would call for Pete and Ricky about nine o'clock, just as it was growing dark.

"You'll know my boat," Mr. Mark told them, "because I'll wink my light twice."

Pam looked disappointed, but she said nothing until she and Pete were pedaling back to the hotel. "Those were nice boys," she remarked, "but I wish they had girl deputies."

"Maybe you can be an honorary member, too," Pete said hopefully.

"I can't do anything brave enough for that," Pam said smiling.

In a short time they had returned the bicycles to the caddy house.

"Oh look," Pam said. "Mother and Daddy are playing golf."

Pete turned to see his parents standing far down on the fairway. Their mother had started her backswing and hit the ball a resounding whack. It flew straight and true, bouncing onto the green.

"They're having fun, too," Pete said, "and leaving the sleuthing to us!"

Pam laughed, and they walked around to the front of the hotel, which faced onto the Gulf of Mexico. Near the shuffleboard court, and shaded by two large palm trees, was a child-sized table and two little chairs. Seated on them were Sue and Holly.

"They are busy making something," Pam said. "I wonder what it is."

The older Hollisters hurried over to the two children. Sue looked up from the table, which was covered with small shells. "We're making earrings for Mommy," she said happily.

"Mother bought us this kit," Holly said, too intent upon her work to look up. In her left hand she held two blank earring backs, and in her right hand a tube of glue. Sue was picking out tiny white shells for her sister to stick onto the backs.

"Where's Ricky?" Pete asked.

"Looking for lion tracks," Sue declared with a sigh.

"Lion's Paws!" Holly corrected, and her tongue peeked out from the side of her mouth as she squeezed hard at the tube of glue.

None came out of the top. Holly's chubby fist tightened and *plop!* a whole blob of glue came out of the bottom! It squirted all over the tiny shells. She quickly put down the tube, and tried to wipe the sticky stuff off them with her fingers. The shells stuck to her hands.

"Don't touch—" Pam started to say, but before she could finish, Sue also had reached her hands into the gooey mess. Now the shells stuck to her fingers too.

Both girls stood up, violently shaking their hands. Then Holly reached down to wipe her fingers on the sandy ground.

"Don't do that!" Pete warned. "It'll only make things worse!"

With tears in her eyes, Holly stood up quickly. In doing so, she bumped into the table. It tilted to one side, cascading the gluey shells down inside the back of Sue's frilly pink sunsuit!

CHAPTER 5

RICKY'S MISTAKE

"Ouch!" cried Sue, as the sticky shells slid down her back. She arched like a bow, wriggled, and waved her stuck-up hands all at the same time.

"Yikes, what is this, some kind of dance?" Ricky asked, running up from the beach.

"It isn't funny," Pam said, then she added, "Holly, Sue, come with me and don't touch anything!"

The two young girls followed their sister obediently to the caddy house. There, Pam asked the man in charge if he had some cleaning fluid.

"Sure have," he replied. "I use it on the soiled golf bags." Then he looked at Sue and Holly in surprise. "Who decorated the girls?"

"It was an accident," Holly said, looking embarrassed.

When the man produced the can of fluid, Pam poured some on a soft cloth and in a short time had cleaned the sea shells off her sisters. Just as she finished, Pam glanced up to see her parents approaching over the green grass.

"Come on, hurry, girls," she said.

"Oh, I won't tell on you," the man said.

"It isn't that," Pam replied. "We still have shell earrings to make!"

The girls gave hurried thanks, then skipped back to the table where Sue and Holly had been working. Pete had repaired the tube of glue, while Ricky had disposed of the sticky shells.

"There is still a lot left to work with," Pam said.

This time the Hollister girls were careful with the glue, and in a short time fashioned a pair of delicate pink and white earrings from the tiny shells. Then they hastened to Pam's room, set the jewelry on the window sill to dry, and changed into dresses for dinner.

Before they entered the dining room, the three sisters went into the hotel gift shop, where the clerk gave them a small box with a fluff of cotton. In this they placed the earrings, and presented them to Mrs. Hollister at the dinner table.

"Oh, you sweet things!" their mother exclaimed. "How lovely!" She reached over to examine Sue's chubby hands and added, "And you didn't get a bit of glue on you, either."

Holly giggled into her napkin while Pam gazed up at the chandelier over the table. Sue dimpled prettily without saying a word. And as Ricky opened his mouth to speak, Pete quickly changed the subject.

"We are going on a beach patrol tonight," he

said, and told about the arrangements he had made with the junior deputy sheriffs.

"I want to go, too," Holly said. "I'm a good detective."

"In Shoreham maybe," Ricky said importantly, "but down here in Florida, it's a man's work."

"I guess it would be pretty dangerous," Mr. Hollister said with a wink at Pam. "I suppose we can leave it up to the boys tonight."

The family strolled along a concrete beach promenade until it grew dusky. When the moon peeked weakly through the mackerel clouds, Mrs. Hollister said, "Come girls, we'll go inside and leave the boys to catch the poachers."

Just then Pete grinned and Ricky saluted sharply, as Bud, Alf and Wyn hurried up to meet them. After the three junior deputies were introduced to the other Hollisters, the five boys set off across the sand.

"Listen fellows," Wyn said, as they proceeded along the pebbly beach. "I think I know how we can trap the poachers."

"How?" Pete asked.

"By making a fake turtle crawl in the sand."

"That's keen!" Pete said. "How shall we make the tracks?"

"By scuffing our feet," Alf replied. "Bud, Wyn, and I practiced it before we came over."

After walking a quarter of a mile along the shore, Pete spied a thicket of palm trees. "Here's a place we can hide," he said. "Could we make the turtle tracks now?"

"Good idea," Alf Cohen said.

The boys walked to the water's edge, then, scuffing their feet in wide arcs, they made a trail to the high part of the beach.

"In the dark that might fool the poachers," Bud Lardner said. "Come on now, let's hide."

The five companions crept into the thicket and lay on their stomachs, resting their heads on folded arms. All was quiet except for the sleepy sound of crickets and the light breeze ruffling the palm fronds.

Pete's eyes roved back and forth across the dark waters.

"I guess nobody's coming tonight," Wyn said.

"Wait, look!" Pete exclaimed softly, pointing down the beach. A light flickered.

"Is that on the shore or from the water?" Bud whispered.

"I can't tell," Wyn replied. "But it's coming closer."

The boys narrowed their eyes and peered over the sand toward the oncoming light. It disappeared, then shone again.

"Maybe it's Mr. Mark's signal," Bud said.

"Or it could be the light of a boat bobbing on the waves," Pete reasoned.

Suddenly a spotlight shone brilliantly on the sand. The boys pressed their faces down hard, not daring to look up into the bright rays coming from a boat only a few feet offshore.

A muffled voice called out. The light went off, and the sound of a keel being pulled over the sand came to the boys' ears. The young detectives looked up to see a light flash off and on as a shadowy figure examined the faked turtle crawl.

"That's our signal!" Ricky said. He jumped up and called out, "Mr. Mark, here we are. Did you find anybody?"

"Crickets!" Pete cried in a husky voice. "Ricky, come back here!" But the exuberant youngster had run halfway across the beach.

"It's a trap!" shouted a man's voice.

"Hurry, we can make it!" cried another.

Now all the boys made a dash toward the water's edge, but not in time to reach the two men. They pushed their boat out into the water, started the motor, and churned off into the darkness.

"Now you've done it, Ricky," Pete said disgustedly.

"But—but—"

"We know you thought it was the signal light," Wyn said, "but you should have waited for us." The moon shone through a rift in the clouds, revealing a downcast look on Ricky's face.

"Don't feel too bad about it," Bud said kindly. "We all make mistakes."

"But not one as bad as that," the redhead declared, and stamped his foot on the damp sand.

"Ricky, come back here!"

In silence the boys walked back to the hotel. They had nearly reached the promenade when the sound of a boat's motor drifted over the Gulf waters. A light blinked off and on twice, and disappeared.

"There's Mr. Mark now, I bet," Pete said.

The boys hastened to the water's edge as the craft came closer. Finally it beached and the conservation man stepped out.

"I chased somebody out there a while ago," he said, "but they got away."

"The poachers, all right," Alf said tight-lipped. "We missed 'em too."

"Well, we'll have to try again, boys," Mr. Mark said. "Thanks for helping."

After the patrol boat had droned out of sight, the three junior deputy sheriffs took their leave. "Maybe we'll see you tomorrow," Pete said.

"Okay, good night," Wyn replied, and they trotted off.

The Hollister boys tiptoed to their room. As their footsteps sounded along the hall, the three girls poked their heads out of Pam's room.

"Did you catch the bad men?" Sue piped up.

"What happened?" Holly and Pam asked together.

Ricky hung his head for a moment, then burst out, "I ruined everything! Even Sue would make a better detective than I am."

Quickly the boys told their story and when they

had finished Pete asked, "Where are Mother and Dad?"

Pam said they had taken a stroll along the beach.

"We must have missed them," Pete said. "Well, good night."

Both boys were fast asleep soon after their heads hit the pillows. How long they had slept Pete was not aware, but suddenly he sat bolt upright as a hand pressed against his shoulder.

"Everything is all right, Pete, don't panic," Mr. Hollister was saying.

"Wha—what's the matter, Dad?" the boy said, as his mother switched on the light in their room. Ricky opened his eyes, then rubbed them sleepily with the back of his hand.

"There is something I would like you all to see," Mrs. Hollister said. "I'll rouse the girls."

"Yikes! What is it?" Ricky asked.

"A turtle! A giant sea turtle!" Mr. Hollister said. "She's crawling up the beach to lay her eggs!"

CHAPTER 6

AN UNWELCOME VISITOR

HEARING the news about the giant sea turtle, the girls were equally excited.

"I want to pet the mama turtle!" exclaimed Sue as she wriggled into her shorts.

"But supposing the poachers find her before we get there?" Pam asked with a worried look.

She was told that Mr. Mark, the conservation man, was guarding the spot. He, too, had seen the turtle and was hiding nearby so that the creature could return safely into the Gulf.

After dressing hurriedly, the children followed their parents outdoors and along the sandy beach.

"There's Mr. Mark," their father said. He pointed to the conservation man crouched in the shadow of a small jetty. It was made of logs driven into the sand. Mark turned around and beckoned them in silence.

"I don't see any turtle," Holly whispered.

Mr. Mark pointed to the high-tide line and said in a low voice:

"She's digging now. Watch carefully." Just then

the moon came out from behind a cover of clouds, lighting the white sand in a dim, eerie glow.

"I see her," Pam said. About two hundred feet from the surf the children could make out the silhouette of the largest turtle they had ever seen. With her hind flippers she was digging a hole, scattering the sand about in all directions.

The youngsters began to whisper questions all at the same time.

"How deep is the hole?" Pete asked.

"And how big are the eggs?" added Holly.

"How many will she lay?" asked Pam.

"One at a time, please," Mr. Mark whispered, smiling.

He told them that the hole would be about two feet deep. "It is narrower at the top than on the bottom," he said. He added that the turtle would lay approximately two hundred eggs. "About the size of Ping-pong balls."

"Will they bounce?" asked Sue.

"Absolutely," the man replied. "I accidentally dropped one on the wet sand and it bounced."

The children looked surprised.

"Really and truly?" Holly asked.

"Yes," said Mr. Mark, "that's the truth."

"Yikes!" exclaimed Ricky. "Bouncing eggs!"

"Now I can see the marks of the turtle crawl!" Pete said, pointing over the sandy stretch. Their eyes, accustomed to the faint light, picked up the tracks made by the creature as she had lumbered to her nesting place.

The youngsters breathed deeply of the fresh salt air. A cool breeze fanned their faces as they watched intently. After the sand had ceased to fly, Mr. Mark said, "Now we will have to wait while she lays her eggs."

Minutes passed and Sue's head nodded. Mr. Hollister cradled the little girl in his arms and soon she was fast asleep.

After forty-five minutes of silence, broken only by the hushed whispers of the children, Pam suddenly said, "Here she comes!"

The turtle's head appeared above the hole. She craned her long neck from side to side. Then her two front flippers appeared and finally the gigantic body emerged from the nest.

"Oh look!" Holly said as the flippers went to work once more. Sand was brushed into the hole and leveled off. Then the turtle went around in circles, disturbing the surface of the beach so that no one could tell exactly where she had laid the eggs. After that the big creature crawled to the water's edge and disappeared into the surf.

"Well, that was some show!" Mrs. Hollister said, rising to her feet.

"The sand is full of eggs and I am full of kinks." Mr. Hollister chuckled, as he rose with the sleeping Sue in his arms.

"Now will the nest be perfectly safe?" Pam

asked as they walked along the beach toward the hotel.

The conservation man told them that sometimes raccoons find the eggs and eat them. "I'll spray the nest tomorrow morning in order to kill the scent of the turtle," Mr. Mark said.

Everybody, including the grownups, slept late next morning. Pam was awakened by a rap on her parents' door and heard the bellman say, "Telegram for Mr. Hollister."

She threw on her robe and went to their room. By this time the others had awakened, too, and trooped in while their father opened the telegram.

"It's from Charlie Tiger Tail," he announced and read, "To the Hollisters: I am in trouble. Await Clementine. Take care."

"Crickets!" Pete said. "What does that mean?"

"And what kind of trouble could he be in?" Holly asked. "He's a nice man."

They all pondered this strange message and Pam said, "Maybe we are to await some word from Clementine."

"That could be," her mother agreed. "We must be patient and see."

After breakfast, Ricky and Pete said they were going to the police station to be sworn in as junior deputy sheriffs. "Then we'll be able to wear the skivvy shirts with the name on them," Ricky said and gave his mother a sly look.

"Oh, I know what you mean," she said and

opened her purse. "Here is some money, Pete. Each of you may buy one."

The boys thanked her and dashed toward the caddy house to rent bicycles.

They sped over the road which bordered the golf course, turned onto the main street and soon pulled up in front of the police station. There they were met by their three new friends and several other junior deputies.

"Everything is all set," announced Bud.

"Come on inside," Alf said.

"Sergeant Reno will swear you in," Wyn declared, hooking his arm into Pete's as they marched into the station house.

"Good morning, Ricky, Pete," the police officer said. "Step right up now and take your oath."

Suddenly from behind them came a rude voice. "What do you mean! They can't be deputy sheriffs!"

Pete and Ricky could hardly believe their ears. They wheeled about to face Joey Brill! He smirked as he came forward.

"I've been coming to Florida longer than these fellows have," he said, "and I'm not a deputy sheriff—so they can't be either."

"Joey Brill!" Pete exclaimed. "How did you ever get here?"

"I told you I was going to Florida," the bully said. "My folks have friends down here."

Sergeant Reno was not the least upset. He looked

amused at Joey and said, "Have you ever made application to join?"

"No, I haven't."

"Then why do you object to the Hollister boys?"

"Because they always make trouble for me."

"That's not true!" Ricky said hotly.

"Let's not argue about it," Sergeant Reno said as Bud, Alf, and Wyn looked on silently. "Pete and Ricky will now be sworn in. Advance and raise your right hands."

Joey watched sullenly as the lawman quoted the oath and the boys repeated it after him. They promised to uphold the laws and act with good sportsmanship.

Then Reno shook hands with the two boys and Wyn, Alf, and Bud slapped them on the back.

"Now can we get our white shirts?" Ricky asked eagerly.

"Sure!" Alf said. "We have them right here in our locker."

When the purchase had been made, Pete turned to Joey Brill. "I hope you have a good vacation down here," he said, "and don't bother us."

"Don't worry!" the bully stormed and strode off.

"How did he know we were going to be sworn in?" Pete asked.

"One of our members lives next door to the place where he's staying," Bud said. "A boy named Tandy. Maybe he told Joey."

Arriving at their hotel, Pete and Ricky proudly showed their skivvy shirts.

"First thing I'll do," Mrs. Hollister said, "is to sew your name tapes inside the collars."

She removed one each from other garments the boys had brought along and quickly stitched them into place.

"Yikes, that's keen!" Ricky declared. "We wouldn't want to lose these, Pete!"

While the brothers tried on their new shirts and admired themselves in a long mirror, Pam, Holly, and Sue went down to the poolside to play with their shells.

"I think this is going to make us better detectives," Ricky said, running his fingers along the words JUNIOR DEPUTY SHERIFF.

Pete, too, threw out his chest proudly. "At least people will know we are on the job," he said. "And look at all the new friends we're making."

Just then through their hotel window the boys heard Holly scream.

"She's calling us!" Pete said. "Come on! Let's hurry."

They leaped downstairs two at a time and ran across the lawn toward the swimming pool. Pam, Holly, and Sue were kneeling beside it, peering into the water. And standing over them was Joey Brill!

"He threw our shells in," Pam said, rising to her feet.

"Why did you do that?" Pete asked.

67

"He threw our shells in!" Pam said.

"It was an accident," the big boy replied. "My foot slipped."

"How did you know we were staying here?" Pete demanded.

"Oh, you have so many *friends*," Joey said, "it's not hard to get information about the Hollisters." He sauntered off around the pool.

By this time Pam was already hastening toward her room. Minutes later she appeared in her swim suit and bathing cap. She dived gracefully into the water and swam along the bottom, picking up the sea shells.

Joey came back to watch as Pam bobbed to the surface and handed the shells to Holly.

"Don't bother the girls any more," Pete warned.

The bully merely grinned as Pam dived to the bottom once more.

"I'm going to get my bathing trunks and help her," Pete said, and started across the lawn.

"So am I," declared Ricky and followed his brother.

Pam came to the surface with another handful of shells. But before she could get a breath of air, Joey pressed his foot on top of her head. Down she went, and came up choking and coughing. As she clung to the side of the pool, gasping for breath, Joey dashed off. Pete and Ricky turned about and sprinted as hard as they could, trying to catch the bully. But Joey's head start got him to his bicycle in time.

"Ha ha, fooled you again," he called out with a sneer as he sped off alongside the golf course.

"Don't come back any more!" Pete called out. "If you do, I'll throw you in the pool myself." He hastened back to see if Pam had recovered from her ducking. Ricky remained behind, shaking his fist at the disappearing Joey.

As the redhead returned along the beach, he met Uncle Dan. The man was swinging his metal detector back and forth over the sand. When he saw Ricky he looked up. "Say, young fellow," he declared, "a couple of men were asking questions about the Hollisters."

"Friends of ours?" Ricky asked him.

"I think not," Uncle Dan replied. "They looked rather rough."

"What did they ask?" Ricky continued.

"They wanted to know who found the turtle poaching spear. Matter of fact, there they are now." Uncle Dan pointed to two men far down the beach. They were so far away that they looked like small specks on the sand.

"Yikes!" Ricky said. "I'm going to find out about them."

Without telling the others, he trotted along the beach. One of the men turned around, and Ricky flattened himself against the sand. Then he rose again and trailed the pair until he was nearly up to them.

When the fellows stopped suddenly, Ricky

jumped into some tall grass near the high-water line and listened as they spoke.

With the wind blowing in his direction, the boy got snatches of the conversation.

"Trouble makers . . . nearly caught . . . outsiders are . . . Tiger Tail."

Ricky immediately realized that these two knew something about the poachers—or perhaps they were the bad men themselves!

"If I could only follow them to see where they live," the boy thought.

The men had drawn closer together and were deep in conversation.

Just then Ricky spied what looked like a Lion's Paw shell several yards away. Warily, he crept out on hands and knees to get it. But as he did, one of the men whirled and saw him.

"That might be one of them now!" the man cried out. Ricky turned to flee, but a moment later was jerked up short by a hand on the back of his collar.

CHAPTER 7

CLEMENTINE'S LETTER

"WHAT'S your name?" demanded Ricky's captor.

The boy looked up into the fellow's face. It was rough and weather-browned. Around his forehead he wore a dirty white kerchief.

Now the other man came forward. He was loose-jointed and walked with a slouchy gait. His straw hat was pulled low, concealing the top part of his whiskery face.

"You heard me!" the first man growled. "What's your name?"

"I won't tell you," Ricky replied defiantly.

"You don't have to," the lanky man put in. "You're Ricky Hollister."

The boy's eyes widened with amazement. "How did you know?" he asked.

"So you admit it," the man added with a sneer. "I can see the name tape inside your shirt."

"Junior Deputy Sheriff, huh!" said the fellow who had Ricky in his grasp. He gave the redhead a shove and the boy fell onto the sand. "Now go away and don't bother us again. Tell your family to mind their own business."

"Yes, go back up North and stay there," the other man said.

Ricky got up cautiously, keeping his eyes on the two rough men. Then he turned and raced along the beach as fast as his legs would carry him.

When he reached the hotel he did not see his brother or sisters out on the sand. He ran upstairs, eager to tell the news of his adventure.

Bursting into his parents' room, he saw the family gathered about a forlorn-looking girl dressed in a bright gown which hung to her ankles. Around her neck she wore several strands of beads. Her black hair was cut short and she regarded Ricky shyly with her wide brown eyes.

"Here is our other son, Ricky," Mrs. Hollister said kindly. "This is Clementine," she told him. "Charlie Tiger Tail's daughter."

"Yikes, how did you get here?" the redhead asked, "and where is your father?"

"She came on the bus, all by herself," Sue spoke up before the girl could reply.

The visitor had arrived only minutes before, Pam explained, bearing a letter from Charlie Tiger Tail.

"I was about to open it," Mr. Hollister said, as he tore one end off the white envelope.

Ricky was impatient to tell about the two men, but he sat cross-legged on the floor and listened to his father, who read:

"I have enemies and advise you Hollisters to stay

"This is Clementine," Mrs. Hollister said.

away from me. Please take care of Clementine for a few days. Your friend, Charlie."

"Goodness, this is serious," Mrs. Hollister said, putting an arm around the Indian child.

"Daddy is afraid that the bad men might hurt Grandma and me," the girl said. "He sent her to a Seminole village and me here. He doesn't want any of you to be in danger, either."

"But we all want to help Charlie Tiger Tail," Mr. Hollister said. "Enemies or not, we'll stay by him."

"Good for you, Daddy," Pam said, as she turned to Clementine. "Are the poachers the enemy your father is talking about?"

Clementine nodded her head yes, and added, "They destroyed the old Seminole camp where we were staying."

"What happened to all the other people?" asked Pam.

"There were none," replied Clementine. "Daddy, Grandma, and I stayed there alone. You see, there are some abandoned Seminole camps around, and once in a while Indians move into them. This one's on Turtle Point and was a good place for Daddy to start his guide trips."

"How was it destroyed?" Pete asked.

The girl replied that while the three of them were out in the jet air boat, somebody had chopped down the group of chickees where they lived.

"But they didn't find our other boat," she said. "It was well hidden in a cove nearby."

"The propeller-driven one, you mean," Pete said.

Clementine nodded. "Everything else is gone," she said, and tears welled into her eyes.

"Don't worry, honey," Pam said, taking her by the hand. "You can live here with us for a while."

"Where did your father go?" asked Pete.

"He's camping about a mile from Turtle Point," Clementine replied. "He has a good hiding place and he'll live there while he hunts the poachers."

Mr. Hollister had the Indian girl draw him a map showing the spot.

"I'm going to find your father," he said, "and give him all the help I can."

After they had eaten lunch in the hotel coffee shop, the tall athletic man rose and said, "I may be gone a few days. Don't worry about me."

The youngsters watched admiringly as Mr. Hollister set off to hunt for Charlie.

"We have a surprise for you, Clementine," Pam told the sad-faced Indian girl. After leading the visitor up to their bedroom, the Hollister girls presented her with the bride doll and its blue outfit. Instantly Clementine's eyes brightened and she smiled. "Thank you!"

"We can play and have fun until your daddy comes for you," Holly said.

Ricky, meanwhile, had given Pete a nudge and beckoned him out into the hall. In the quiet of their own room, the redhead told his brother about his trouble with the two rough men.

"I didn't want to interrupt Daddy for fear he would change his mind about looking for Charlie Tiger Tail," Ricky said. When he heard the fellows' description, Pete snapped his fingers.

"Crickets!" he exclaimed. "Those are the two men who stole the spear from me. I think we should tell the police."

The boys first told their mother, and with her permission set off for the station house. Upon arriving there, they walked up to the sergeant's desk.

After giving a snappy salute, Pete said, "Junior Deputy Sheriffs Pete and Ricky Hollister reporting, Sergeant Reno."

"More clues?"

"Yikes, you bet!" Ricky said, and told what had happened to him.

The officer promised to redouble the search for the poachers. Then he thanked Ricky for being so observant.

The redhead grinned and said, "I guess that makes up for the other day when I scared the poachers off."

"Sure does," said Pete.

The brothers jumped on their bicycles and were headed back to the hotel, when suddenly around the corner sped Joey Brill on his bike.

"Ugh!" said Ricky, wrinkling his nose.

Joey pedaled alongside Pete and said, "I'm going to be a deputy sheriff too."

"Good," Pete said. "Glad to hear it."

"You're not glad at all!" Joey declared. "You want to hog all the glory yourself."

"Why don't you let us alone and go your way?" Pete asked quietly, keeping safely to the edge of the street.

The hum of rubber tires continued as the three boys rode on silently for a while. Then the road bent around a small swampy pond.

Joey stood up on his pedals and urged his bike part way ahead of Pete's.

"An old trick," the Hollister boy thought to himself. "Joey pulled it in Shoreham once. He's going to cut me off."

With a mischievous gleam in his eyes, the bully pulled his bike sharply to the right. At the same time Pete applied his brakes and the wheels did not touch.

Startled by his failure, Joey made the mistake of glancing back. His bicycle veered off the road and plowed into the marshy pond.

Head over heels went Joey! He came spluttering up with weeds dripping down over his forehead.

Pete could hardly keep a straight face. And Ricky laughed out loud.

"See what you did to me!" Joey stormed, as he reached into the shallow water for his bicycle. "I'll get you for this!"

"Enjoy your swim," Pete said.

The Hollister boys pedaled off, chuckling all the while. Ricky was so happy that he started to zigzag from one side of the road to the other.

"Look out or you'll take a spill, too," Pete warned. At the same time, faintly in the distance came the sound of a racing motor. This was followed by a siren's wail which grew louder and louder.

Pete and Ricky veered to the side of the road and stopped. A police car came into sight. When the driver saw the two boys he pulled to a screeching stop beside them.

"It's Sergeant Reno!" Pete exclaimed.

"Hop in, fellows!" the officer commanded.

The boys laid their bicycles in the high grass near the edge of the road, jumped into the car, and slammed the door shut.

"I think we've got the poachers!" Reno said, as they sped off again with the wailing siren sending a chill through Pete and Ricky.

Half a mile farther, the officer turned into a lane, bumped along the rough ground, and came out on the beach.

Far down the shore another police car, its red light blinking, headed toward them. Between it and Reno's car, two men fled along the hard-packed sand.

CHAPTER 8

BIG LULU

SEEING Sergeant Reno's car, the two men turned and raced in the opposite direction. But they were hemmed in by the other police vehicle which bore down on them.

Finally the men stopped running and stood still while Reno's prowl car pulled up beside them on the sand.

"Oh, yikes!" Ricky said, as the sergeant opened his door and stepped out. "Those aren't the poachers."

"You're right," Pete agreed. "These aren't the fellows who took the spear from Pam and me."

"Who are you? And why are you running?" the policeman asked the men, who tried to appear nonchalant with their hands in their pockets. A couple of officers had stepped out of the other car and, with Pete and Ricky, circled the strangers.

Both were sun-tanned and unshaven. The taller one wore a battered straw hat and gave his name as Bama Crosset. The other, who wore a soiled white cap, said he was Terry Madison.

"We're beachcombers and we're hitchhiking North from Miami," Bama explained.

"We had a report that two suspicious characters were working their way along this beach," the sergeant said. "Why did you run away from us?"

Terry shrugged. "We were just nervous, I guess."

"Stand against the car so I can search you," Sergeant Reno ordered. The men did as they were told. They had nothing dangerous concealed about them, but the officer found their pockets filled with small pieces of jewelry and trinkets.

"Where did you get these?" Reno asked.

The men insisted that they had found the articles while beachcombing on the east coast.

"Crickets!" Pete said. "Wait a minute! That looks like the stuff Uncle Dan had in his house."

"The man with the metal detector?"

"That's right," Ricky put in. "He lives down the beach aways, too, just where these two men were coming from."

"The kids are balmy," Madison said, trying to laugh off the suspicion.

"Come with us," the patrolman ordered. "We'll see."

But before Reno could put the suspects in the back of his police car, Uncle Dan himself came running along the beach. He reached them, breathless.

"My house has been burglarized!" he exclaimed.

"Are these the missing objects?" Reno asked, putting the trinkets on the automobile hood.

"Those are mine, all right!"

"Then we have the fellows who looted your place," the policeman said.

The prisoners grumbled, then grudgingly admitted that they had seen the front door of the beach cottage open, had walked in, and helped themselves.

The missing property was returned to Uncle Dan, and Sergeant Reno put the other two patrolmen in charge of the prisoners. "Take them in and book them," he said, and the captives were hauled away.

Then the officer turned to Ricky and Pete. "Come on, I'll take you back to your bicycles," he said, and added, "we didn't get the poachers, but we did trap those petty thieves." He explained that sometimes a clue on one case can lead to an entirely different bit of mischief.

"You boys are fine junior deputies," he said. "Keep up the good work."

The sergeant let Pete and Ricky off where they had hidden their bicycles. The brothers said good-by and pedaled back to their hotel, bursting with news of their adventure. At dinner that evening, talk centered about the exciting events of the day.

"Have you heard from Daddy yet?" Ricky asked.

"No, but I think it's too soon to expect a call," his mother said. "Now that we have Clementine with us, why don't we all relax for a day and have some fun together?"

"Like what?" asked Sue, tilting her chin.

"Like going to the Everglades Zoo," Mrs. Hollister replied with a smile.

She said that the hotel manager had told her about the unusual zoo, several miles away.

"It has most of the Florida animals in it," she added. "Some of them I'm sure that only Clementine has seen."

"The hammocks are full of wild animals," the Indian girl said.

"They sleep in hammocks?" Holly asked, looking confused.

Clementine's brown eyes twinkled. A hammock, she explained, was an island in the marshes. "You'll be surprised when you see all of our animals," she said. "I'd like to go to the zoo."

"Then let's do it," Pam said.

Next morning Pete and Ricky were playing catch with a red rubber ball near the swimming pool when their mother and the four girls came out of the hotel.

"Ready for the zoo trip?" Pam called out.

Pete grinned, faced about, and lobbed the ball to her. Pam caught it expertly and tossed it back to Ricky, who stuffed the ball in his back pocket.

"A cab is waiting for us," their mother said.

All hastened to the front of the hotel and squeezed into the taxi. It did not take long to arrive at the outskirts of town, where a large sign directed them to the Everglades Zoo.

Mrs. Hollister led them into a low building, paid the admission fees, and walked to the rear, emerging onto a large garden area. Scattered among the tall trees were deep pits. Ricky was first to reach the edge of the nearest one.

"Yikes!" he cried out. "Alligators, thousands of them!"

Resting in a shallow pool were dozens of sleepy-looking reptiles, some on top of others. A few had their mouths open. Many lay with their snouts under water, only their bulging eyes protruding.

"Step this way!" called a cheerful young man. "I'm your guide," he continued. "If you'll follow me, I'll tell you all about our friends at the Everglades Zoo."

After gazing at the crocodiles, the children watched a tank full of turtles, as other sight-seers attached themselves to the group.

"Here is a funny turtle," the guide said. "This one flicks out his red tongue under water and when the little fishes come up to investigate—snap!—he has his dinner."

"Oh!" said Sue, shrinking back. "Is it his dinner time yet?"

The sun beat down hotter as they walked along the winding path. Holly liked the small Florida deer in a broad enclosure and Ricky admired the huge owls. As he circled behind their cage, one big fat owl turned its head all the way around.

"He's got eyes in the back of his head!" Ricky chuckled. "Like my teacher at school! She sees all the tricks we're doing."

Next was a cage with two fierce-looking panthers. They padded back and forth, their yellow eyes glaring. As the children watched, fascinated, one of the beasts came to the front of the cage and snarled.

"Crickets!" said Pete. "How'd you like to be out in the swamp and meet *that* face to face!"

Holly shivered.

"You see it can be dangerous in the Everglades," the guide said.

"Look at the raccoons!" Pam called out, coming to the next enclosure.

The little animals, with their funny masks, scampered about, looking curiously at the sight-seers.

"I didn't know you had raccoons in Florida," Pete remarked.

"Thousands of them," the guide replied. "They are little bandits too, if you don't look out."

Then the young man raised his hand and said, "We have another wild creature in the zoo which is not from Florida, but Big Lulu likes the warm weather and is content to stay here."

He pointed down the path to a deep pit, in the center of which was a pool of greenish water. Beside it stood a huge hippopotamus.

"Big Lulu is very friendly."

"Big Lulu is very friendly," the man went on, "if you're friendly toward her."

As the group pressed on to look at the hippo, Holly tugged Pete's arm. "See who's coming," she whispered.

Pete turned and saw Joey Brill walking toward them. He had on a junior deputy sheriff's shirt which appeared to be three sizes too small for him.

"Look here," he said when he reached the Hollisters. "They made me a member."

Clementine, who up to now had walked quietly beside Pam, held her hand to her face and giggled.

"What's so funny?" the bully demanded.

As he did so, a woman, holding a small towheaded boy by the hand, walked up to Joey angrily.

"Give my son back his shirt!" the woman said. She held out a brown one which evidently belonged to Joey.

"It was a fair trade," the bully said. "I gave him my shirt, he gave me his."

"You forced him to do it," the woman said.

"Yes, he made me," her son spoke up.

"O.K., Tandy," Joey said with a scowl. "You went back on your bargain."

"It's too small for you anyhow," Holly chirped up.

Joey took the brown shirt, went behind the owl cage and stripped off the small white skivvy. He returned with his own shirt on and handed the other to little Tandy. Then without a word he walked in back of Ricky and snatched the red rubber ball from his pocket.

"Give that back," Ricky demanded.

Instead, Joey tossed the ball at the hippopotamus. It hit Big Lulu on the nose and she gave a surprised grunt.

The ball bounced around the pen, coming to rest alongside one of her huge feet. With that the hippopotamus lay down, covering the ball completely. The guide turned to scold Joey, but the bully had fled.

"I'll get the keeper," the young man said. He whistled to a gray-haired attendant standing on the other side of the hippo pen. "Big Lulu is sitting on a rubber ball," he said. "Will you get it for us?"

The keeper bent down and picked up a long pole which lay beside the pit. Then he reached out and prodded the hippo. Big Lulu merely wriggled her tiny ears. The man tickled her sides. She only grunted. Then the attendant hastened off and returned with a morsel of hay, which he attached to the pole and held it under the huge beast's nose. Lulu munched it but did not get up.

By this time the sight-seers were laughing.

"Looks as if Lulu has decided to sit all day," the keeper said. "Come back tomorrow and I'll have your—"

"Pretty please, Big Lulu!" Sue's little voice sounded clear above the hubbub. As if by magic, the hippo lumbered to her feet and slid into the green water of the pool.

The onlookers cheered when the keeper retrieved the ball and gave it to Ricky.

Upon returning to the hotel, the children donned their swim suits. Pam loaned an extra one to Clementine and they all raced to the sandy beach.

"You're like the otters at the zoo," Mrs. Hollister remarked, as she swam among them with clean graceful strokes. Then she stood up in the water, shook the drops out of her hair and asked:

"How would you like a cook-out on the beach for supper?"

"Yikes!" Ricky cried out. "That'll be keen! We can collect driftwood."

"May we have hot dogs?" asked Holly.

"And hamburgers, too?" put in Clementine. "That's what I like."

When their romp in the surf was over, the young swimmers stood under a shower near the promenade before hastening back to the hotel.

When they had put on clean clothes, Mrs. Hollister ordered supplies for a picnic supper from the hotel kitchen. Soon the food was delivered to their room in a big wicker hamper.

With Clementine and Pete carrying the basket, the happy family marched along the beach, in the opposite direction from the place where the sea turtle had laid her eggs.

After a while they came to a grove of palm trees above the high-water mark.

"Here's a good spot to have a fire," Ricky said, running forward to a small depression in the sand.

"Fine," his mother agreed.

The girls quickly spread a cloth, while Pete and Ricky gathered wood. By the time the sun started to sink toward the sparkling horizon of the Gulf of Mexico, they had the blaze going brightly.

When the embers were just right for cooking, frankfurters were speared on wooden skewers and the hamburgers clamped in little metal holders.

"Hmm, this is good," Pam said as she nibbled a juicy hamburger in a white bun.

Each child had his own bottle of soda. As the rim of the crimson sun dropped out of sight the youngsters drew closer to the fire.

Darkness came fast and the embers glowed like little cherries as the children began gathering up their picnic belongings.

Mrs. Hollister had just packed the cloth into the hamper when Clementine clutched Pam's sleeve and said, "I hear a rustling noise." She pointed toward a clump of palm trees. The others stopped and listened.

"Maybe it's a wild animal," Ricky whispered.

Pete walked forward bravely, scooped up a handful of pebbles, and threw them into the heavy undergrowth around the trees.

Suddenly two figures slipped out of the thicket!

CHAPTER 9

A PLACE MARKED X

"So THERE you are!" came a cheery voice as two men approached the picnickers.

All of the children cried out, "Daddy!" because the two men were Mr. Hollister and Charlie Tiger Tail.

Clementine flung herself into her father's arms. "I'm so glad you're safe!" she said, snuggling her head against his shoulder.

"Yikes, you scared us!" Ricky said.

Mr. Hollister explained that upon their arrival at the hotel they had been told about the picnic. "So we walked through the trees at the edge of the beach until we heard your voices," he said.

"What about the bad men?" Holly asked.

As they strolled back along the sand, Mr. Hollister told how he had located Charlie in his camp.

"We scouted around on foot last night and most of today," he said, "but we found no trace of the poachers."

"They may have moved up the coast for a while," the Indian remarked, "but they'll come back to Turtle Point because they think I'm gone."

"And we'll be waiting for them when they turn up, won't we, Dad?" asked Ricky stoutly.

"Yes," declared Mr. Hollister. "We came to Florida to help Charlie, and we're going to do just that."

"Besides," Pete added, "we're already in this case up to our necks!"

They decided to obtain a room at the hotel for Charlie that night and to start in the morning for Turtle Point. There the Hollisters would help make a new chickee.

"It'll be fun living Indian-style," Holly said.

"We can explore Santabella and Captive Islands," added Ricky, "and look for Lion's Paws."

"We'll try to solve the mystery of the weird noise, too," Pam said. "Can you tell us more about Captive Island, Charlie?"

"It used to be a pirates' hideout," the Seminole replied. "The buccaneers would kidnap rich ladies and hold them captive there until ransom was paid."

"How exciting!" Holly exclaimed. "I wish we'd meet some fierce pirates."

Early next morning, after everything had been packed, the party set off for the Everglades. Pam asked to ride with Clementine in the Seminole's pickup truck. The others drove with Mr. Hollister.

After several hours they reached the small town of Everglades where they stopped at a drugstore for lunch. There Charlie Tiger Tail picked up his trailer which he had left at the gasoline station for safe-keeping.

For a while the travelers proceeded along the main highway, then turned onto a narrow sandy road which followed the wooded coastline.

Charlie Tiger Tail's truck bounced along in the lead, pushed its way through an overgrown trail, and finally stopped on a point of land which jutted out into the Gulf. Offshore lay two small islands fringed with red and black mangrove trees.

"The one on the left is Santabella," Charlie said, as they all alighted from the vehicles. "And the other"—he pointed—"is Captive."

As the tide was high, the two islands were separated by a narrow band of water.

"Let's go over there right away," Ricky said impatiently.

"First we'll have to build the chickee," his father told him, "and you can help."

"We'll gather palmetto fronds for the thatched roof," Clementine volunteered.

Several wrecked chickees stood before them in a clearing surrounded by low, thick-growing palmetto trees. Fortunately, the supporting poles had survived the raiders' attack. Charlie and Mr. Hollister picked the least damaged and began to frame the rest of the dwelling while the youngsters gathered strips from the small palms.

"We don't have all these trees in Shoreham," Pam remarked, as the Seminole was thatching the roof of the open-air dwelling.

Charlie explained that many kinds of trees grew in this nearly tropical climate. "On the hammocks you will find gumbo-limbo and sea-grape trees." Then he looked down thoughtfully at the children and added, "If you ever go to Captive Island be careful of the manchineel tree. It's poisonous."

"Oh dear!" Mrs. Hollister exclaimed. "How will we know it?"

The Indian explained that its fruit were shaped like apples and that it affected human beings like poison ivy. "Even the smoke from a burning man-chineel tree is dangerous," he cautioned them.

"Gumbo-limbo, gumbo-limbo," Sue said, dancing around. "What a pretty name."

"I need one more bundle of palms," Charlie called down from the roof.

"I'll get it for you, Daddy," Clementine said. She dashed off into a thicket, with Pete at her side. Together they pulled off armfuls of branches from a low palmetto.

As Clementine bent down to scoop up some fallen fronds, she touched a cold metal object. "Look, Pete!" she exclaimed.

The boy dropped his bundle to examine the find. "It's an ax head," he said. "And it's been broken off the handle."

"Do you suppose it's a clue to the men who wrecked the chickees?"

"Could be," said Pete as he stuffed the broken tool into his belt. "I'll show it to Dad."

Pete and Clementine handed their bundles of palmetto to Charlie. Then they showed the ax head to Mr. Hollister.

"It hasn't rusted very much," he said.

"Which means it has been here only a few days," Pam remarked.

"Say, wait!" Pete exclaimed. "Look over here."

He directed their attention to one of the poles on a ruined chickee. Near the base were several fresh nicks made by an ax.

"No wonder all the poles are standing," Charlie remarked as he slid off the thatched roof. "Someone tried to cut them down, but the ax broke."

"Where did you children find this?" Mr. Hollister asked.

Pete and Clementine led everyone to the palm thicket and pointed to the place. They all searched the ground for more clues.

Suddenly, Sue spied a piece of folded paper peeking from beneath a clump of long grass. "I found a picture!" she cried, waving it toward the others.

Pete took the paper from her hand and exclaimed, "It's a map!"

"Of Santabella and Captive islands," Charlie added, looking over his shoulder. "One of the poachers must have dropped it."

"It's a map!" Pete exclaimed.

While walking back to the chickee, Pete examined the drawing closely. On the far end of Captive Island was marked a small X. "It could be a coincidence," the boy thought and put the paper into his pocket.

With their shelter completed, the Hollisters helped Charlie get folding cots from his truck.

"I hope you don't mind roughing it," said the Indian.

"Don't worry about us," Ricky declared. "We're pioneers."

The raised platform of the chickee had not been damaged, and the camp beds were put in neat rows. While Pam and Holly made them up with clean sheets, pillows, and blankets, Mrs. Hollister cooked dinner over an open fire. By the time they had eaten, evening was coming on and Charlie led his guests to a secluded cove nearby.

There, beneath low, overhanging trees, were the Seminole's two air boats. The new one with the jet engine now had a two-way radio next to the driver's seat. Beside the old propeller craft lay a large rowboat.

Although Ricky and Holly begged for rides, they were told it was too late. "When the sun sets, it becomes dark very quickly on the water," Charlie said.

On the way back to their camp, Pete and Ricky walked slowly, inspecting the trees for ligs. Soon the sun was only a red sliver on the horizon and the boys had fallen behind the others, who were out of sight.

"We'd better catch up," said Ricky.

Pete turned to glance toward the cove. Startled, he saw a person's head disappear behind a tree.

"Come on, Ricky!" he whispered, and dashed back.

There was a crashing noise in the bushes as someone tried to get away. Pete and Ricky pounced and brought down a boy of about Pete's age. He was thin, sun-browned, and had a thatch of blond hair. His big eyes were wide with fright.

"Who are you?" Pete asked. "What are you doing here?"

The boy said that his name was Larry LeBuff, and he lived on Santabella Island. He was the son of a fisherman.

"Were you spying on us?" Pete asked.

The boy nodded his head.

"Why?" asked Pete.

"My dad was out in his boat this afternoon and saw you come," he answered softly. "I just wanted a look at you."

"Well, why didn't you come right up to us and say hello?" Ricky demanded. "We wouldn't bite you."

Larry looked down shyly and did not reply.

"I'm sorry we jumped you," Pete said. "We thought you were one of the poachers." Then he quizzed the boy about the sabotage of the Seminole chickees.

"I saw three men in a boat that night," Larry told him. "I spied their lights offshore. They were wandering around the hammocks, too. Probably fire hunters, Dad said."

He explained that fire hunters were men who shone lights into the eyes of wild animals, then killed the blinded creatures.

"That's awful!" Ricky exclaimed and Larry nodded.

Just then Charlie Tiger Tail called, and they saw him hastening toward them. Noticing that the two boys had not come into camp with the others, he had gone back to the cove.

The Hollisters told him what had happened.

"Do you know this boy?" Pete asked.

"Yes," the Seminole replied. "And his father, too. They are good people. Talk a little longer if you like," he added. "I know you're all right, so I'll go back."

When he had left, Pete and Ricky began to tell Larry about themselves. Finally the blond boy said that his boat was not far away and that he must return to Santabella.

"Before you go," Pete said, "I want you to look at this." He pulled the map from his pocket. "Is there anything particular about Captive Island where this X mark is?"

"Yes. A great big boat on dry land."

"Will you take us to see it?" said Pete.

"No! I'm—I'm afraid to," Larry replied fearfully.

CHAPTER 10

MIDNIGHT SHIVERS

"What's there to be afraid of?" Pete asked. "The strange noises?"

"I can't tell you now," Larry replied. "See you tomorrow if I can make it," he added and ran down to the beach.

Pete and Ricky watched him pull a rowboat from some tall grass, launch it into the water, and row toward Santabella Island. Then the two boys rejoined the rest of the family at the camp.

As they stepped into the chickee, Charlie Tiger Tail was lighting a gasoline lantern. The Seminole Indian grinned. "At dark we all go to sleep," he said, pointing to the line of cots.

When the campers had located their belongings, Charlie put out the light, and all prepared for bed. Each person had a flashlight tucked beneath his pillow.

The night noises lulled the children to sleep. But Pam, who never slept as soundly as the others, was awakened in the middle of the night by an odd sound. She lifted her head from the pillow and listened. "Someone is snoring," she thought. "Who could it be? Daddy? Charlie Tiger Tail?"

Then, she realized that the noise was coming from outside the chickee. She reached over to the next cot and touched Clementine's hand. The Indian girl was awake at once.

"Someone is sleeping out there in the thicket," Pam whispered into her ear. "Hear him snoring?"

"That's not a person," Clementine replied softly.

"What is it then?" asked Pam.

In the darkness the Seminole girl replied, "You'd never believe me if I told you. You'll have to see it for yourself. Get up and follow me."

Pam had no idea what Clementine meant, but she trusted her new friend. Sitting up quietly on the edge of the cot, Pam slipped her feet into her shoes, and took out her flashlight. Hand in hand the two girls stepped down from the platform of the chickee. They did not flash their lights until they had felt their way some distance from the thatched hut.

"Clementine, what are you doing?" Pam asked, holding tightly to the Seminole girl's hand.

By this time the snoring had grown even louder.

"Don't be afraid," Clementine said, as she headed directly into the brush from where the sound came.

Creeping along softly, they came to a small pool of water. Clementine shone the light on the greenish surface of the pond. A tiny head and two bulging eyes protruded.

"Is that it?" Pam asked.

"A frog!" Pam exclaimed. "Is that it?"

Clementine giggled and said, "This is a snoring frog. People from the North are often fooled by it."

"What a tenderfoot I am!" Pam exclaimed and grinned. The frog kicked and vanished, leaving a little circle of waves which spread to the edges of the small pond.

"Come, we must hurry back before the others find us missing," Clementine said.

They had not gone far before Clementine stopped short. "Listen!" she said.

"Another snoring frog?" Pam whispered.

"No, I think it's a motor."

The girls turned off their flashlights, and faced toward the beach. Halfway between Turtle Point and Santabella Island, a light moved along the water to the muffled sound of a motorboat.

"Hurry, we must tell Daddy!" Clementine exclaimed.

The two girls ran stumbling through the underbrush and reached the chickee out of breath.

After they had given their fathers the alarm, the rest of the campers woke up also.

"That can be nothing else but the poachers!" Charlie said. He raced to his truck and returned with two huge flashlights. He and Mr. Hollister ran toward the beach with all but Sue and her mother following.

Not until they reached the water did the men turn on their powerful lights. The beams swept back and forth over the wave tops but nothing could be seen except the white crests skimming toward the sandy beach.

"Are you sure of what you saw?" Charlie asked the girls.

"Oh yes, Daddy," Clementine replied.

The lights were doused. The searchers stood still, listening, and looking toward the two islands which loomed black in the dim moonlight.

"Maybe they landed and are hiding," Pete remarked.

Charlie Tiger Tail said that the poachers would act only in secrecy. Once they knew that someone was looking for them they would flee, and await their chance some other night.

Starting back toward the chickee, the group was suddenly startled by a weird sound. Everyone stopped short to listen.

"Somebody's screaming!" Pam exclaimed.

"No," Pete said. "It's more like a wild animal howling."

"Yikes," Ricky whispered, and shivered.

The eerie noise sent chills through them all as it drifted across the water from the islands.

"That's the sound I was telling you about," Charlie Tiger Tail said softly. "It comes from Captive Island, I'm sure."

"Maybe the men in the boat are making it," Holly suggested.

"No," the Indian replied. "It's coming from far

away." After a few moments more, the fearful sound died and they hastened on to the chickee. There, little Sue was clinging to her mother. They, too, had heard the spooky noise.

"What do you think it was?" Mrs. Hollister asked her husband.

"I don't know," he replied. "I've never heard anything like it before."

As they all went back to their cots, Ricky took Pete aside. "We can find that odd noise, Pete," he said.

"How?"

"Larry knows all about these islands," Ricky went on in a low voice. "Maybe he can lead us on the search."

"Good idea," Pete replied. "We'll ask him in the morning."

The youngsters wakened to smell bacon frying over the campfire, and by the time they had dressed, a delicious breakfast was awaiting them.

After the last bit of scrambled eggs had been eaten by the hungry children, Charlie Tiger Tail directed the boys to a fresh spring not far from the chickee. Pete and Ricky each took a pail, and returned with water for the girls to wash the dishes.

"Charlie and I are going to scout along the coast in his jet air boat," Mr. Hollister said. "We'll be back later."

Pete quickly told of the plan to visit Larry Le-Buff on Santabella. "We can look for shells there and maybe do some sleuthing ourselves," he added.

Mr. Hollister glanced at the Seminole with a questioning look.

"That's all right," Charlie said. "They can take our large rowboat. The water between here and the islands is calm enough today."

Mrs. Hollister and the girls quickly packed sandwich lunches for everyone.

"Sue and I will look for snoring frogs," Mrs. Hollister said gaily, as the others trooped off behind Charlie to the cove.

The two men set off first. Then Pete and Ricky pulled the rowboat into the calm water and manned the oars. Clementine sat in front as navigator, while Pam and Holly took the rear seats.

The boys pulled with even strokes, although Pete had to let up occasionally so as not to go in circles, because Ricky was not so strong as he.

They made good time across the open water. When the Santabella beach ground beneath their keel, Clementine sprang out of the boat and helped to pull it onto the sand. Larry came out of a grove of palm trees and walked shyly to meet them.

"Hi," he said.

"This is a dandy island," Pete replied, looking around.

"What beautiful shells!" Holly cried out.

"See this lovely Murex," Pam said, bending down for the spiny creature.

Within a few minutes the girls had picked up a

perfect Chinese Alphabet, Angel Wings, and a small Lion's Paw.

"Oh, I could stay here forever!" Holly said, her eyes dancing with excitement.

Pete reminded them that they had detective work to do. "Did you hear the queer noise last night, Larry?" he asked.

"It made me shiver," the island boy answered.

"Did it come from Captive Island?" was Ricky's question.

When Larry nodded, Pete said, "What about this big boat?"

The blond lad hunkered down on the sand, and with a splinter of driftwood made a diagram as he told the Hollisters a strange tale.

"There was a rich man who liked Captive Island. He also liked Mississippi riverboats. So he bought an old one in New Orleans," Larry said, "and had it towed across the Gulf."

Then, the boy explained, workmen dug a canal several hundred yards into the island. The steamer was hauled in, and the canal filled up again with sand. "So there the boat sits," Larry said. "It's a huge one and has a steel fence built all around it."

"Does the rich man live there?" Pete asked.

He was told that the owner had died shortly after his project had been completed. "I understand the place is for sale," Larry went on. "Only a caretaker named Mr. Dodd lives there."

"Let's go see it!" Ricky said as Larry rose to his feet again.

The boy shook his head. "Not to Captive Island," he declared.

"Oh, come on, Larry," Pete said. "We'll all stick together."

"After all," said Pam, "you never hear the noise in daylight, do you?"

"No," he admitted, then added, "I guess it'll be all right."

"Shall we take our boat?" Pete asked.

The blond boy shook his head. "It's shorter to cut across this island," he told them.

With Larry in the lead they made their way in and out among palmettos and scrubby gnarled trees.

Pete and Pam walked together, carrying the lunch basket.

"This strange riverboat might be a good clue," Pete said quietly.

"To the poachers?"

"Maybe. It might also have something to do with the strange noise. Who can tell what—"

"Ouch!" screamed Holly, as her left foot sank into a hole and she fell to the ground.

CHAPTER 11

THE GUMBO-LIMBO

LARRY ran back to Holly. "You stepped into a gopher hole," he said, and helped the pigtailed girl to her feet.

"Are you hurt?" Pam asked, examining Holly's ankle.

"No, but it surprised me."

The children gathered around the hole. "See?" Larry said. "This was made by a Florida gopher turtle. Holly stepped right on top of the tunnel and broke it in."

The shy boy was beginning to feel more at home with the others and explained that these land-turtles' burrows were sometimes as long as forty feet. "And all kinds of animals live in the gopher tunnels," he added.

"Like what?" Pete and Pam wanted to know.

Larry told them that harmless indigo snakes, burrowing owls, skunks, and many insects used the turtles' dwelling for their home, too.

"Then we shouldn't disturb it any more," Pam

said kindly. She picked up a fallen palm branch and put it over the hole.

"Now Mr. Gopher Turtle won't get sunburned," Holly declared with a grin, and skipped along ahead of the others.

After a long walk they reached the far side of the island and ran along the beach to the tip of Santabella.

"The tide's going out," Larry said. "We should be able to wade over to Captive in half an hour."

The time was spent in gathering more unusual shells. When the water was low enough, the children kicked off their shoes and waded to the neighboring island. At the edge of the beach was a cluster of trees. There in the shade of a mangrove, they left the lunch basket and their shoes.

As they walked along the beach, Pete said to Larry, "I wonder who made that map and why the X was marked on it."

"I don't know," the boy confessed. "Mr. Dodd is a nice old man. He waves to me and Dad sometimes when we go by in our fishing boat."

The sand was white and hard beneath their bare feet, and occasionally Ricky and Holly stomped along in the shallow water.

Presently they came to a bend in the shoreline. Ahead two smokestacks loomed up above the trees.

"Crickets!" Pete called out. "Larry, those must be part of the riverboat."

"What do you want?" he demanded roughly.

"Yes," the boy replied. "Aren't they big?"

Soon the whole steamer came into sight and the youngsters stopped to gaze at it. The enormous white boat was three decks high with a small wheelhouse tucked between the two black stacks. At the stern was a huge paddle wheel.

Pete and Larry walked ahead toward the high wire fence. They had to stand on tiptoe to peer over the bushes growing on the inside of the enclosure.

Pete reached up, grasped the links of the fence, and was just about to haul himself up for a better look, when the bushes directly in front of him parted and a man's face appeared.

"What do you want?" he demanded roughly. "Stand where you are!" The man hurried along beside the fence, unlocked a gate, and stepped out to confront the youngsters.

He was short and pudgy with a bald head, bushy eyebrows the color of the sand, and a small mouth above his double chin. A smile flicked on and off his face as he talked. Now his voice was almost a purr as he asked, "You're looking for somebody?"

"I thought we might see Mr. Dodd," Larry said.

"I'm his assistant. My name is Seeber. Mr. Dodd is not here at the moment."

"My friends and I were just looking around," Larry went on. "I wanted to show them the riverboat."

The man smiled quickly again. "Look at it all you want," he said, "from outside the fence. But don't climb it, will you, boy?"

"No sir," Pete said.

Seeber waddled back toward the gate, then hesitated and turned his head. "Were you looking around here last night?"

"No," Pam said.

"Me neither," Larry added.

"Why do you ask?" Pete inquired. "Did you see some other children?"

The man told them that he had heard someone on the beach. "Shell hunters, I guess, or maybe prowlers," he added.

"Turtle poachers I bet!" Ricky declared. "They've been around here."

"I advise you to be careful," Pete told the assistant caretaker. "We found a map. Look here."

He reached into his pocket and pulled out the paper with the X mark on it. Seeber took it in one hand, and with the other stroked his bald head thoughtfully.

"Maybe your place has been marked for a robbery," Pam ventured.

The plump man chuckled silently and his shoulders shook. A quick little smile appeared and then vanished. "Robbery? Why, there is nothing here to rob."

"They can't take your boat away." Ricky laughed.

"Then maybe it's a good place to steal turtles," was Pete's guess.

"Say, you children think of everything," Seeber remarked, regarding them with admiration.

"We're trying to solve a mystery," Pete said, then suddenly asked, "What about these weird noises?"

The man's bushy eyebrows waggled, and he put his fingers to his lip. "Don't mention it!" he said.

"Did you hear them last night?" Larry asked.

The man nodded. "No good will come of it," he went on. "The sounds are bad! They come from somewhere on Santabella."

"Oh no," Larry said. "I know they don't because I live there."

"And where do you live?" Seeber asked the Hollisters.

The children told of the new chickee which they had helped Charlie Tiger Tail to build.

"Oh yes, the Seminole," Seeber said, as he shuffled through the gate again. "Mr. Dodd has told me about him. Fine man." He locked the gate, slapped at a fly on his head, and disappeared on the overgrown path which led to the riverboat.

"What do you make of him?" Pete asked Larry when Seeber was out of earshot.

"I don't like him as well as Mr. Dodd," Larry said. "I wonder why he needed an assistant."

"That's a big place to keep in order," Pam said. "If Mr. Dodd is old he might need some help."

The youngsters walked beside the wire fence, careful not to touch it. The superstructure of the old paddle-wheeler loomed white and glistening above the shrubs and trees.

"There's someone in the wheelhouse," Larry said, pointing up to it.

"It's Mr. Seeber!" Holly exclaimed, as a bald head ducked out of sight below the window.

"He has his eyes on us, all right," Pete said. "Let's go back to the shore."

"Okay," Larry replied. "Maybe next time we can find Mr. Dodd."

"Yikes, I'd like to see the inside of that old boat," Ricky said, hopping on one foot to the water's edge.

As they strolled along the curving beach, the youngsters stopped here and there to pick up odd-looking sea shells.

"What a wonderful collection to take home," Pam remarked. "We can put them up in little bags to sell at The Trading Post."

As they approached the tree where they had left the lunch basket, Ricky said, "I'm hungry. Let's eat!"

"Not on the beach. It's too hot," Holly protested, wiping little moist beads from her forehead.

"I know a good place," declared Larry. His eyes twinkled as he led them into the grove.

"See the ligs!" Pam cried, running up to one of the tree trunks.

The beautiful creatures glistened in the sunlight that sifted through the branches.

"They are pretty," Larry said, surprised that the Northerners knew something about the Southern snails. "But come over here to this tree. It's nicer to sit under."

Pete fetched the hamper while Pam and Clementine spread a red-and-white checkered cloth over a smooth spot.

"What an odd tree," Pete remarked, looking up.

"It's a gumbo-limbo and it is a strange one," Larry replied, turning his head. Only Clementine saw him wink, and she remained silent.

"In what way is it strange?" asked Pam.

Larry pretended not to hear, and picked up a white stone, which he whipped through the air. It rolled along the beach and glistened in the broiling midday sun.

"Come and get it!" Pam called to Ricky and Holly. They ran from a banyan tree, which both were trying to climb at the same time, and sat cross-legged beneath the gumbo-limbo.

As they ate cold-meat sandwiches and drank lemonade, an odd thing began to happen. Steam oozed from the branches and drifted down on the youngsters.

"Yikes! The tree's on fire!" Ricky exclaimed, jumping up with a half-eaten sandwich in his hand.

"Am I seeing things?" asked Pete, as he put down his paper cup.

Larry and Clementine laughed. "I hoped it would happen," the island boy said. "Not many people get to see this." He told them that only on the hottest days gumbo-limbo trees give off vapor.

"It can't hurt you," Clementine said. "But come, let's sit under the banyan tree."

By the time they had finished eating, the gumbo-limbo had stopped steaming.

"It's time for me to go home," Larry said. "I've some chores to do for Dad."

"We'd better go back, too," Pete said.

Together they forded the shallow water to Santabella.

"Thanks for showing us your islands and the riverboat," Pete said.

Larry nodded. "Thank you for the lunch," he replied. "Can you find your way across the island?"

"Sure."

"Then I'll leave you here," Larry said. "Goodby," he called, as he ran down the beach. The Hollisters and Clementine put on their shoes and began walking toward the place where they had left their boat.

"This is more of a mystery than ever," Pete told Pam.

"Captive Island sure is a queer place," the girl agreed. "Did you like Mr. Seeber?"

Pete shrugged. "He's all right, I guess. And he's scared of those noises, too."

Watching for landmarks, Pete led the way past the gopher hole. Soon they reached the sandy beach facing Turtle Point.

Pete peered up and down the coast. "Hey!" he exclaimed. "Where's our boat?"

"It's gone!" wailed Holly.

CHAPTER 12

AN ODD WARNING

"WHERE could our boat be?" asked Pam, looking puzzled.

"The tide may have carried it out," Pete ventured. "We should have pulled it higher onto the sand."

"Where's the exact spot we left it?" Clementine asked, as she paced along the beach.

"This is it, I think," Pete replied, walking behind her. "Here's the mark of the keel on the sand."

"Look!" said Ricky. The others gathered around to see. "Footprints!"

The boys bent down to examine two sets of tracks which headed toward the palm trees at the edge of the sand. Between the prints was a deep gash, apparently made by their boat's keel.

"Crickets!" Pete declared. "Somebody dragged it off toward those trees."

"A joke of some kind, I'll bet," Ricky said. "Do you suppose Dad and Charlie were over here trying to fool us?"

But Pete's face was serious. With the others at

his heels he followed the trail in the sand to the palm grove. He shouldered his way through the broken underbrush, then suddenly stopped and pointed up into a palm tree.

The boat was hanging suspended from the top by its anchor rope. It swayed gently in the breeze, about five feet off the ground.

"That's no joke!" Pam cried out.

"I'll say it isn't," Clementine agreed. "See what's painted on the bottom."

"Yikes!" Ricky cried out. "A skull and cross-bones."

They ran closer to examine the boat. Underneath the pirate's insigne was printed the word: BEWARE.

The youngsters quickly surmised that someone had been watching them cross to Santabella Island. While they were making their way to Captive, their enemies had hauled the boat off and hoisted it into the palm tree as a warning.

"It's frightening," Clementine said. "I wish my father were here."

Ricky volunteered to untie the rope. Pete gave him a boost, and he shinned up the tree. While he loosened the rope at the top, Pete and Pam held on to the rowboat. When the line fell to the ground, the others helped ease the craft onto the sand. In a few moments Ricky was down beside it.

"Wait!" Holly said. "Where are the oars?"

"They must be somewhere around here," Ricky said.

The youngsters searched about in ever widening circles. They found the anchor lying in the underbrush, but the oars were nowhere around.

"Daddy's initials were on them," Clementine said. She told the Hollisters how she had helped her father to burn CTT onto both blades.

"This is a fine predicament," declared Pam, making a wry face. "Now what will we do?"

"We'll have to find Larry again," Pete said, "and use his boat to get home."

Grasping the gunwales tightly, the youngsters hauled the rescued craft back onto the beach. They left it there while they crossed the island in search of Larry's house.

After a long trudge they finally saw the fisherman's cabin set well back from the shore in a grove of palm trees. They ran up to it calling out Larry's name. The boy appeared at the front screen door, a startled expression on his face.

"What happened?" he asked.

When Pete told him, the fisherman's son looked worried. "More mysterious happenings! Don't worry. I'll get you back to Turtle Point." He hastened into the house and came out with a small outboard motor.

The Hollisters and Clementine followed him to where his rowboat lay on the sand. Larry quickly attached the motor, pushed the boat into shallow water and beckoned the others to climb aboard. When they did, it sank nearly to the gunwales.

"Sit very still," Larry warned as he started the motor.

The trip around the island was slow, and the passengers were afraid to take a deep breath for fear of rocking the overloaded craft. Even though they sat perfectly quiet, little splashes of water flicked into the bottom. All breathed a sigh of relief when Larry finally sighted their rowboat on the beach and steered toward it.

"Now we can manage all right," he said, as they landed.

Larry tied Charlie Tiger Tail's boat behind his own. Then Pete and Ricky pushed it into the water and hopped aboard, taking Pam with them. Now that the cargo was divided, the youngsters felt safe as they putt-putted across the channel toward Turtle Point.

"Thank you, Larry," Pam said after they had reached the shore and untied Charlie's rowboat.

"If you find the oars let us know," Pete said.

"Okay," the island boy promised and turned his boat toward Santabella again.

"Can you come back and play with us tomorrow morning?" Ricky asked.

"All right! See you then," he answered and waved good-by.

Back at the chickee, the campfire was lit and Mrs. Hollister was starting supper. The grownups were amazed to hear what had happened. Mr. Hollister and Charlie Tiger Tail had been cruising among the hammocks in the Everglades, but had not circled Santabella and Captive that day.

"I'll bet the poachers have a hideout on one of the islands," Pete said, "and they hung up the boat to warn us away."

"Our enemies are very bold," the Seminole remarked.

"But they can't give us the slip forever," Mr. Hollister declared.

"We'll get 'em yet, Dad!" Pete vowed.

Soon the aroma of broiling hamburgers filled the air and they ate supper.

When it was over Sue hopped up and went to her father. "Now may I tell?"

Mr. Hollister nodded, laughing.

"We're going to have an air-boat race," Sue announced.

"Yikes!" exclaimed Ricky, dancing about like an Indian. "I want to ride with Charlie."

"Me too!" cried daredevil Holly.

"That wouldn't balance the boats right," the Seminole said. "Suppose that Ricky and Pam ride with me. Pete and Holly, you can go with your father."

The youngsters raced on ahead to the hidden cove and hopped into the air boats.

"John, I think it only fair that you have a head start," Charlie said.

"Fine! How about ten boat lengths?"

"Agreed," Charlie said, as he started his jet motor.

With a loud bang and a plume of black smoke, Mr. Hollister got his propeller spinning. The two boats eased out into the water, where the men decided on a race course one mile south to a group of hammocks on the Gulf shore. They would circle the first island and return to the starting place.

After Mr. Hollister took a good lead, Charlie waved his hand as a starting signal and both boats sped off in a whirlwind of noise.

"Come on, Dad!" Pete cried.

Mr. Hollister applied a full throttle and white spray flew out from both sides of the zipping air boat. Holly turned to look back, her pigtails flying in the breeze.

"He's gaining on us, Daddy!" she shouted.

Close behind, Ricky and Pam braced themselves in the front seat as the wind almost took their breath away.

After Mr. Hollister had made a neat turn around the hammock and headed back, both boats drew abreast. The youngsters looked at each other and could only grin. They were holding on too tightly to wave!

For a quarter of a mile the boats raced along, Charlie's craft whining like a banshee and Mr. Hollister's roaring like a lion. Then the jet began to prove her power. Foot by foot she pulled ahead of

The boats whined and roared along.

the propeller-driven craft. At the finish line Charlie was well in the lead.

"He beat us fair and square," Pete said as both eased into the cove.

"Fastest thing in the Everglades!" Mr. Hollister said with a wave to the victor.

Sue stood on the shore holding Clementine's hand. "I want a ride too," she pleaded. "In the whistly boat."

Charlie grinned. "All right, hop in."

Sue and Clementine stepped into the boat.

"And may I go too?" Mrs. Hollister asked.

"Yikes, Mother wants to ride!" Ricky said, as he helped her step aboard.

As it was not a race this time, Charlie did not push his motor to top speed. Instead, he took them sight-seeing among the hammocks. In places the passages were narrow and overhung with dense mangrove foliage.

The Indian leaned forward from the driver's seat and said, "Clementine knows these water trails. She's rowed in here many times."

Suddenly Sue cried, "Look out, Charlie, we'll bump!"

The Indian swerved his air boat in time to avoid what appeared to be a log floating on the water.

"It's an alligator!" Mrs. Hollister exclaimed, as the reptile flicked his tail and disappeared beneath the surface.

Charlie stopped the boat. "That was a crocodile,"

he said. "Did you notice the narrow pointed snout? An alligator's would be more blunt. There aren't many crocs around here any more. This may be a female with a nest nearby."

As her father spoke, Clementine noted their location.

"We should look for a nest," Charlie said, "and protect it, especially if the croc has already laid her eggs."

But it was getting too dark to do any exploring. The Seminole guided his boat back to the cove. When he had told the others of their adventure, Pam said, "I'd love to see a crocodile's nest."

Clementine smiled and said nothing. As she went to bed that night, she moved close to Pam's cot and whispered into her ear.

After breakfast next morning Larry returned to play with Pete and Ricky. Pam nodded at Clementine. The two girls strolled into the palmetto foliage and made their way quietly to the cove.

"I told Daddy what we're going to do," Clementine said, "so don't worry." She took a paddle from her father's air boat, adding, "We'll use this in the rowboat."

With Clementine paddling, they made their way into the maze of small islands. The narrow waterways were gloomy, though here and there sunlight slipped through the branches and dappled the dark water. In places strands of Spanish moss hung down, curtaining the banks.

"Please don't get lost," Pam whispered, as they made their way quietly forward.

"I'm taking a short cut to the place where we saw the crocodile," Clementine assured her.

After a while the Indian girl said softly, "This is the spot. Now we'll look for a nest. It shouldn't be far away."

The dip, dip of the paddle was the only sound as the boat glided through the shallow water. The Seminole girl looked right and left with keen eyes. Finally she said, "I see crocodile tracks on that muddy bank." She steered the boat close to the shore.

Pam saw the dark claw prints, and an odd pile of twigs and leaves nearby. She was about to ask Clementine what this was, when suddenly a chill ran through her. There was no breeze, yet a long strand of moss moved ever so slightly. As she listened intently there came the rippling of water. Someone was hiding in the swamp not far from them!

CHAPTER 13

THE INDIAN VILLAGE

SUDDENLY there was a whining sound followed by the roar of an airplane propeller. At the same time a blast of wind struck the girls' faces and rocked their little craft.

"An air boat!" Pam cried out. "And it's getting away!"

"The poachers again, I'll bet!" said Clementine. "And we can't catch them."

Pam replied that the girls were lucky that *they* had not been caught. Whoever it was, she reasoned, may have thought that Charlie Tiger Tail and Mr. Hollister were trailing them.

As the Seminole girl turned the rowboat about, Pam got a closer look at the crocodile nest of twigs and leaves. Several eggs, a little larger than chicken eggs, lay scattered about.

Then Clementine gasped. "Look Pam! The mother crocodile!" Near the raided nest, and camouflaged by the underbrush, lay a crocodile about six feet long. The reptile was motionless, its eyelids were half closed.

"Why didn't she protect her nest?" Pam whispered.

"Maybe she's dead," replied Clementine. The girl pushed the boat closer to the scaly creature.

Next to the crocodile lay a broken oar. The initials CTT had been burned into the blade.

"They hit the poor thing, that's what they did," Clementine said, "and with Daddy's oar!" Now the girls knew for certain that it was the poachers who had followed them and painted the skull and bones to warn the Hollisters.

"Oh, they are mean to hurt the mother crocodile!" Pam said sternly. "I hope she's still alive."

Her friend leaned forward and touched the animal's tail with her paddle. It switched back and forth with such force the blade was nearly knocked from the girl's hand. The crocodile turned its head and opened its yellow eyes balefully.

"Let's get out of here!" Pam exclaimed.

But Clementine did not have to be urged. Using all her strength, she paddled the rowboat as fast as possible through the tangled Everglades waterway.

Pam glanced back over her shoulder, fearful that the stirred-up reptile might chase them. But soon they were out of sight of the looted nest and no crocodile had showed in the rippling water.

Both girls heaved sighs of relief, and with steady strokes, Clementine made her way back to Turtle Point.

The companions found their families eating a

lunch of broiled fish which the boys had caught during the morning. Larry had left a few minutes before. All were astonished when they heard of Pam and Clementine's close call with the poachers. The menfolk determined to press their search for the crocodile-egg robbers that afternoon.

"If we can locate their camp we could lie in wait for them," Charlie Tiger Tail said. Immediately the youngsters begged to go along. After thinking it over, the Seminole agreed.

"We can turn this into an outing for all of us," he said.

The plan was to search the area around the crocodile's nest, then continue deeper into the Everglades and visit the Seminole village where Clementine's grandmother now lived.

Mrs. Hollister, Pam, and the two younger girls went in Charlie's jet air boat. Ricky, Pete, and Clementine accompanied Mr. Hollister. With Charlie's craft in the lead, the boats traced their way among the hammocks until they came to the rifled crocodile nest.

The boats stopped. "Old mother croc has vanished," Charlie said, as he stepped onto the spongy ground. He put the scattered eggs back into the nest and covered them with leaves. The Seminole picked up the broken oar, and found its mate nearby.

"Two men must have tailed the poor crocodile." Then he added, "Oh-oh, there she comes!"

The others looked to see a snout and two eyes surface in the waters behind them. Charlie Tiger Tail hopped into his boat and both crafts went on their way again, leaving the reptile to guard her few remaining eggs.

In and out of the waterways sped the air boats. Sometimes the openings among the mangrove roots were as wide as a street, and in other places no broader than a sidewalk. Finally the lead boat emerged into a small lake. On the far side of it stood a group of chickees.

"That's Grandmother's village!" Clementine said, clapping her hands.

As the voyagers drew closer they could see women and children, in colorful costumes, busy about the chickees. One elderly woman with a brown, wrinkled face approached the dock with swinging steps, the hem of her dress nearly touching the ground.

Charlie Tiger Tail maneuvered his boat so that Mr. Hollister could land first. Out hopped Clementine into the arms of her grandmother. "We brought some friends with us," she said, smiling as Pete and Ricky stepped ashore.

When Charlie's boat had unloaded, all the Hollisters were introduced to Grandmother Tiger Tail. She fingered the many strands of beads around her neck and nodded at each of the visitors.

"I'm making dresses," the Indian grandmother

said. She beckoned to the girls. "Come, let me show you."

Holly, Pam, Clementine, and Mrs. Hollister followed the old Seminole woman to her chickee. There, mounted on a small table in the shade of the thatched roof, was an old-fashioned sewing machine. Spread upon it was a voluminous skirt of many colors.

As the girls watched fascinated, the grandmother's deft fingers guided the material under the whirring needle. Holly was fascinated by the treadle which rocked back and forth under pressure from the old woman's foot.

Sue, meanwhile, held onto her father's hand while he, Ricky, and Pete walked through the Indian camp with Charlie Tiger Tail.

"It must be fun to live here," Sue chirped, looking right and left at the colorfully dressed people.

"It is," an Indian boy spoke up. He was Pete's age, and not as shy as some of the other children who gazed at the visitors from a distance.

"Hello, Jim," Charlie Tiger Tail said, and introduced the boy to the youngsters. Jim had a round face, black eyes, and a wide, ready smile.

"Do you want to see a real dugout canoe?" he asked them eagerly.

"Yikes! I'll say so!" Ricky replied.

While Mr. Hollister and Charlie walked on, the Seminole boy led the three children to another dock. Beside it floated a long wooden canoe. Pete immediately saw that it was a log which had been scooped out and the ends tapered.

Jim picked up a long pole lying on the dock and said, "Step in, but be careful. This is a Seminole dugout canoe. It's tippy."

Pete went first, holding his hand out to steady Ricky and Sue. Easing themselves down, they sat in the bottom. Jim stood in the stern, and poled the canoe slowly out into the lake. With strong strokes he sent it speeding over the calm waters.

"Crickets! This is fun!" Pete declared. "Could I try poling it once, Jim?"

The Seminole boy nodded, circled about, and came back to the dock. There Pete took the pole and pushed the boat through the shallow waters.

After making a circle Pete returned to give Ricky a try. The red-haired boy did well, although he had trouble pulling the pole up out of the muddy bottom as he went along.

Up until now, Sue had done nothing but gaze delightedly about her. But as Ricky brought the boat back to the dock, she sang out, "Now it's my turn."

"But you're too small," Ricky protested.

"I was little last year. I'm big now," Sue said, her lower lip in a pout.

"I'm afraid you can't even hold the pole, Sue," Pete said kindly.

But she would not take no for an answer. Smiling

"Crickets! This is fun!"

sweetly at Jim, she cocked her head. "May I, pretty please?" she asked.

"All right," he replied. "But in a child-size dugout."

Jim directed Ricky to another wooden dock, beside which lay a little canoe. "This is what the children practice in," he said, as they all stepped out of the large craft.

While Pete and Ricky steadied either end of the small dugout, Sue stepped in and took a little pole which Jim gave her.

"You'd better go with her, Ricky," the Indian boy said. The redhead sat down in the bottom of the canoe and Sue pushed it away from the dock. When they had glided several boat lengths into the lake, Sue's eyes twinkled and she said, "I'm going to give it a real hard push."

She dug the pole into the lake with all her might. But she could not pull it out again!

Holding onto the pole tightly, Sue was lifted out of the canoe as it slipped away from under her. She dangled over the water, clinging to the pole and screaming!

CHAPTER 14

A DARING PLAN

"Help!" Sue screamed as she slipped lower on the pole. Her feet nearly touched the water as the small Indian canoe drifted away.

Ricky knelt in the bottom and paddled furiously with both hands, reaching Sue as she was about to slide into the water.

Grasping the pole with one hand, he pulled the little girl into the dugout with the other.

The onlookers, standing on the lake shore, clapped and shouted as Ricky managed to get the pole out of the mud and guide the craft back to shore.

"I didn't see what happened," Pete said with a wink as the youngsters stepped out of the canoe. "Do it again, will you?"

"You looked like a pole vaulter," declared Mr. Hollister as he swept Sue up into his arms. Then he gave Ricky a pat on the back for his quick thinking.

"Sue, come with us," Pam said. "We have something to show you."

Mrs. Hollister and the girls returned to Grandmother Tiger Tail's chickee. The Seminole lady had made a small multicolored blouse, which she gave to Sue. The little girl pulled it over her head and pirouetted about.

"For the rest of you, I have beads," the Indian grandmother said. She reached out and put strand after strand of beautiful shell beads over the heads of Holly, Pam, and Mrs. Hollister.

While the girls were admiring their gifts, Pete, Ricky, and Jim chatted at the dockside. "How would you like to play a game?" asked their new friend.

"Yikes, what kind?" said Ricky.

"I'll get a head start and you try to catch me," Jim replied. "I'll be Billy Bowlegs."

"Who's he?" asked Pete.

Jim explained that Billy Bowlegs had been a famous Seminole Indian chief. "When he ran into the Everglades the enemy could not find him," Jim said with a grin. "You won't find me, either."

"Oh yes we will," Ricky said, "'cause I'm going to make-believe I'm an FBI agent."

"I'll yell when I've had a good enough start," Jim said. "I'm Billy Bowlegs and here I go!" He bounded through the tall grass behind the chickee and disappeared into the brush.

"Yee-ow!" Jim called out, and Pete and Ricky took after their quarry like hounds chasing a rabbit. They dashed through the waist-high grass, in and out among the moss-laden trees toward the center of the hammock.

"Yikes!" Ricky said. "He's vanished like a ghost!"

"He must be around here somewhere," Pete said. "He didn't have that much of a head start."

The brothers searched all the way to the opposite shore of the island and back again. But they found no trace of Jim.

Near the edge of a thicket, Pete sat down on a log and Ricky sprawled on the ground beside him.

"Let's give up and call Jim," suggested Ricky, mopping his freckled brow with a handkerchief.

"Billy Bowlegs! We give up! Where are you?" Pete shouted between cupped hands.

Suddenly the log moved! Then it flew into the air, sending Pete backward head over heels. Underneath it was their friend Jim!

"Crickets!" Pete exclaimed, scrambling up. "You scared us. How did you get under that log?"

The Seminole boy grinned. "That's not a log, it's my little dugout canoe," he said. "It's a good place to hide."

"It sure had us fooled," Pete said. "That gives me an idea, Ricky. We could take this canoe back to Santabella Island, and hide under it to watch for the poachers."

Quickly he explained to Jim that the Hollisters were helping Charlie Tiger Tail track down the bad men.

The Indian boy said they could borrow his dugout. "You'd be more comfortable, though, if you dug a trench in the sand first, then put the canoe over your heads."

Their talk was interrupted by Mr. Hollister calling, "Come, boys! We're leaving now!"

Pete and Jim carried the dugout to the dock, where they placed it in the jet air boat.

"What's this?" Mr. Hollister asked, and chuckled when told about the youngsters' scheme.

"All right, I guess we can take it with us," Charlie Tiger Tail said.

Mrs. Hollister and her three daughters were saying good-by to Grandmother Tiger Tail and Clementine, who had decided to stay in the Indian village for a few days.

"She can help me with my sewing," the old lady said. "Clementine is very good at it."

In the air boats once more, the Hollister family and Charlie skimmed through the narrow waterways, then along the shore until they reached Turtle Point.

"Look, we have a visitor," Mr. Hollister remarked as the two air boats glided into the cove.

Waiting on the shore beside his motorboat was Mr. Mark, the conservation man. He stood up and waved at them.

"I thought maybe the poachers had captured you all," he said as the air boats slid up onto the sandy beach.

"Hello, Mark," Charlie said. "What brings you down here?"

The wild-life agent said that poachers had been active farther north the night before. He had chased them, and they had fled south toward the Everglades.

"They were here all right," Charlie replied. "Clementine and Pam surprised them robbing a crocodile's nest."

"Where they disappear to is a mystery," the man said. "But we know that they have a fast air boat."

"We'll have to press our search all the harder," Mr. Hollister declared.

"And speaking of that," Mr. Mark said, "the police have another search on their hands. A boy named Joey Brill is missing."

"What!" Pete exclaimed.

"We know him," said Holly.

The conservation man told them that Joey had been gone for two nights. The Shoreham bully had been seen thumbing a ride along the road toward the Everglades.

"Goodness, I do hope they find him," Mrs. Hollister said.

"Oh dear," Sue put in, "maybe a crocodile will nip him."

"I don't think Joey will dare go into the Everglades," Pete said with a shrug. "Maybe he stopped at one of those Indian villages along the highway."

Mrs. Hollister invited the conservation man to have supper with them. When it was over, he left, saying that he was going to take his motorboat farther down into the chain of islands to look for the poachers.

"And we're going to post a watch on Santabella Island," Pete said, as he walked with Mark to the cove.

"Good luck," the government man said. He stepped into his boat, and turned off into the twilight toward the darkening hammocks.

When Pete trudged back to the camp he found his father and the others in front of the chickee. "Dad," he said, "why don't you and Charlie join Ricky and me on our watch tonight?"

"You beat me to the question," the Seminole said, looking admiringly at the boys. "Your father and I have this thing all worked out."

Hearing Mr. Hollister explain their scheme, Pam and Holly begged to take part. "No," Mrs. Hollister said. "Someone will have to stand guard here at the chickee. That's our job."

After dark the moon rose like a giant tangerine, sending ripples of light across the Gulf of Mexico.

Pete and Ricky each took a flashlight, then stepped into the jet air boat with their father and Charlie. In no time at all they circled around Santabella, landed, and helped to pull the craft out of sight into a dense thicket.

Following their plan, Mr. Hollister and Charlie

took posts some distance from each other in the grove of trees behind the wide sandy beach. Pete and Ricky, carrying the wooden canoe over their heads, reached a point near the water's edge, midway between the two men. Then, digging like turtles, they scooped out a large hole in the sand. After that they jumped in and pulled the dugout over their heads.

"Yikes, this is keen!" Ricky said. "It's like a seashore hut."

Here and there the brothers scraped away sand from under the edges of the canoe, making slits so that they could look out over the beach. Pete also made a larger hole at the back in order to signal his father and Charlie with the flashlight if necessary.

The long wait started. Now and then Pete shone his light on his watch as minute after minute ticked by. Meanwhile, the tide crept up on the sand, inch by inch.

"We can't stay here too long," Ricky said, "or we'll get all wet."

Pete admitted that he had not thought of this when they had dug the pit so close to the water, but they could not dig another farther up on the sand for fear of exposing their position.

Pete was looking down the beach and Ricky up, when suddenly both boys exclaimed at the same time, "A sea turtle!"

Only seconds apart two giant reptiles clambered

They dug like turtles.

out of the waves. They were clearly visible in the bright moonlight. The brothers could even see the two crawls distinctly as the turtles lumbered halfway up the sloping beach. There they stopped, and the sand flew from beneath their flailing flippers. The nest holes grew deeper and deeper as Pete and Ricky looked on awe struck.

But suddenly the boys felt cold water trickling into their hiding place.

"Yikes, look, Pete!" Ricky exclaimed. "The sea is almost on us."

The water lapped little holes along the edge of the overturned canoe, but the boys did not dare to move. They might frighten the turtles. As they waited, clouds slid over the moon, making it hard to see any distance.

Suddenly Ricky's heart lurched with excitement. He tried to speak, but words stuck in his throat. He could only tug his brother's arm and point in the darkness toward the Gulf waters. The dim shape of a boat hit the beach not more than twenty feet from them.

Two men hopped out and raced toward one of the turtle nests. There they crouched on the sand, observing the giant reptile covering the eggs which she had laid.

"We'll signal Dad and Charlie," Pete whispered into Ricky's ear. He reached for his flashlight at the bottom of the pit. It was wet! So was Ricky's! They would not light!

Pete moaned softly. "Now what'll we do?"

The big turtle which the poachers had singled out for their prey started lumbering down toward the water. The two men sprang at it, and tied a rope around one of its flippers.

"We have to do something!" Pete exclaimed. "Come on!" They threw the dugout from over their heads. Yelling like Indians, both boys sprang up and made a dash for the two men.

"Dad! Charlie!" the boys shouted.

The poachers spun around, their jaws agape with surprise. Roughly they pushed Pete and Ricky to the sand, then continued dragging the sea turtle toward their boat. Pete rose again with Ricky at his side. Desperately, the boys flung themselves onto the rope. In the distance they heard the shouts of their father and Charlie Tiger Tail. They were coming!

CHAPTER 15

CALLING A COPTER

As RICKY clung to the rope tied around the sea-turtle's flipper, he looked up into the faces of the two angry poachers. One was short, with close-cropped hair and a blond beard. The other was tall and had the largest hands Ricky had ever seen.

The big fellow grasped Pete and Ricky with one hand and sent them spinning onto the sand. But in doing this, he let the rope slip off the turtle.

The short man cried out and tried to wrestle the reptile as she lumbered toward the water's edge. He was no match for the huge creature. Once in the surf, she vanished into the safety of the Gulf waters.

Seeing Mr. Hollister and Charlie bounding over the beach, the poachers jumped into their boat, started the motor, and got away.

"Yikes, Daddy! The sea turtle escaped!" Ricky shouted in triumph when the grownups reached them.

"Are you hurt?" was their father's first question.

"Just bruised a little," Pete answered. "That tall man had hands like hams."

"Then I know who he is," Charlie declared. He explained that the poacher must be Ham Cedars, a ruffian who claimed to be a Seminole. "But he isn't an Indian at all," Charlie added hotly. "He gives us a bad name."

Ham Cedars, the Hollisters learned, usually operated farther down the coast, where he was the ringleader of a lawless gang. Charlie felt certain that he must have a hideout in the Everglades not too far away. "My guess would be," he said, "that Ham's using an abandoned Indian village."

Praising the boys for their good work, the two men walked beside Pete and Ricky, with Charlie carrying the dugout over his shoulder.

They returned to Turtle Point in the air boat, told their story to Mrs. Hollister and the girls and soon were fast asleep.

At daybreak the Hollisters and their Indian friend prepared for a long search. Only Sue and her mother were to remain in the chickee.

After lunches had been packed, the sleuths set off. As the hot sun rose over the small islands, the two air boats zigzagged through the narrow waterways.

Since he knew where the old Indian villages were located, Charlie took the lead. The searchers stopped first at one abandoned camp, then another. Nobody was in sight, and an examination of the chickees showed that they had not been used in a long while.

Finally, Charlie slowed his boat and maneuvered through a small stream, where thick roots and leafy branches caused everyone to bend low. Soon they emerged into a little lake encircled by hammocks lying close together. Across from them, on the biggest island, a thin plume of smoke drifted into the air.

"Look!" Pam exclaimed softly. "We've found the poachers!"

"It could be," Charlie said, shutting off his engine. "That's an abandoned camp." He signaled Mr. Hollister to stop his motor, and the two men paddled quietly to the nearest end of the large hammock.

"What'll we do now?" Ricky whispered, as they all stepped ashore.

Charlie Tiger Tail said that he would radio for a Coast Guard helicopter. Then they would steal up on the camp to make sure that the poachers did not escape. The Seminole spoke over the two-way radio and was told that a whirlybird would arrive shortly.

Cautiously, the searchers picked their way across the hammock. Finally they reached the open place where three chickees stood. In front of one, a fire was burning, but nobody was in sight.

"Maybe they've gone already," whispered Pete.

"Come with me," Charlie said. "We'll check the shore to see if we can find a boat."

Leaving the others to watch the camp, Charlie

and Pete pushed quietly through the palmettos and tall grasses until they reached the overgrown mangrove shoreline. But they could not follow it because the matting of intertwined roots was too thick to penetrate without using an ax.

The Seminole turned and beckoned Pete to accompany him into the water. Both kicked off their shoes, skinned off their shirts, and stepped into the lake. Using a side stroke, the Indian swam quietly along the shore with the boy behind him. For a hundred yards there was no sign of a boat. Suddenly, however, Pete spied a movement in a small cove and whispered, "Look over there!"

The bow of a canoe inched out. One person was in it—a boy.

"Joey Brill!" Pete exclaimed, nearly gulping a mouthful of water. Then he called out loudly, "Hey, Joey! Wait!"

Charlie and Pete swam quickly into the cove and pushed the canoe back to land. Joey was so surprised and scared that he stepped out onto the ground, shaking all over. "Wha—how—gee whiz!" was all he could say.

Having heard Pete's shout, the others raced across the clearing toward the cove. Soon Joey was surrounded.

"What are you doing here?" Charlie asked, as he and Pete climbed dripping onto the hammock.

"I ran away," Joey confessed, "because you Hollisters were having all the fun in the Everglades.

I wanted some too." He told how he had hitch-hiked to a fishing village, then rented a canoe and set off along the waterways with a small supply of food. "I was only going to camp out one night," he explained, "but I got lost."

"It's just lucky we found you," Pam said.

"I'm glad you did," Joey replied, hanging his head. "I was scared."

"Your mother and father might never have seen you again," Holly scolded. "They must be awfully worried."

Joey admitted that he had done a foolish thing, and glumly walked back to the chickees with his rescuers. Just as they entered the clearing a noisy helicopter hove into sight. The palm-tree branches swirled and swayed beneath the whirling rotors as the copter landed alongside the chickees.

The pilot stepped out. "Did you get the poachers?" he asked.

"No, but we found the lost boy, Joey Brill. You can take him back with you," Charlie said.

"Okay, deputy," the pilot replied, gazing up at the sky. "I'd better not waste a minute," he added. "Looks like a storm brewing." He ushered Joey into the copter.

"At least I'm having *some* fun," the bully said grinning, and he waved good-by as the craft took off.

After Pete and Charlie had recovered their shoes and shirts, everyone returned to the air boats.

"The pilot was right about the storm," Charlie said. The sky was darkening and wind lashed the quiet water into little whitecaps.

No sooner had the party reached Turtle Point, than rain began to fall and gusty wind whistled over the beaches.

The family huddled in their chickee until dark, when the storm let up.

"It'll be a good day for shelling, tomorrow," Charlie said as they got ready for bed. He explained that the large waves washed up beautiful and unusual shells from deep in the Gulf.

Next day, after the two men had left to scout around the hammocks to the north, the children and Mrs. Hollister rowed across to Santabella Island. They took a picnic lunch and wore swim suits under their play clothes. After frolicking in the surf all morning, they ate hungrily. Then while Sue, Holly, Ricky, and their mother hunted shells, Pete and Pam made their way to Larry's cabin.

"Hi," said the fisherman's son, as he ran out to meet them. "Did you have any luck with the poachers?"

"No," Pete replied, and told what had happened.

"Let's go look at the riverboat," Pam said. "Maybe the wind blew it out to sea again," she added with a wink.

The three trotted along the beach, and crossed the shallow water to Captive Island.

"Oh look!" Pam said, when they sighted the

paddle steamer. The two tall stacks had been blown over by the storm. The gate stood open.

"I wonder where Mr. Seeber is," Pete remarked, walking toward the enclosure.

"I think something's wrong," Pam said. "Maybe he got hurt when the stacks fell over."

The three children walked through the gate and closed it behind them. Then they began to circle the huge stern-wheeler.

"I wonder how you get into it," Pete said.

"There's a door in the front," Larry replied. "Follow me."

The island boy trotted along, but suddenly ducked into a clump of bushes and pulled Pete and Pam in with him. "I saw somebody!" he whispered.

Crouching low, the three peered toward the riverboat. In a doorway stood Ham Cedars and the fellow with the blond whiskers. They scowled and stared at the spot where the youngsters were hiding.

"I'm sure I saw them!" Ham said gruffly and pointed. "Right over there in the bushes!"

The two men set off on a run directly toward the children's hiding place.

"We can't stay here!" Pete whispered. "Come on!" The trio dashed out and raced for the gate.

"There they are! Get 'em!" Ham Cedars cried.

With the pursuers so close behind, the children had no time to open the gate. Instead they ran around to the other side of the riverboat, with Pam screaming for help.

"I think something's wrong," Pam said.

Although the men were big, they were not as fast as their quarry. Pete, Pam, and Larry circled the boat. There was no place left to go except into the doorway. Larry dashed in first. Pam followed. Pete was last, with the angry, shouting poachers not far behind. He jumped inside and slammed the door.

CHAPTER 16

THE TRAP DOOR

THE children found themselves in an ornate lobby. An elegant spiral staircase led to the upper deck. As they pounded frantically up the carpeted stairs, the poachers burst through the door below.

"Stop! Come back here!" Ham Cedars shouted, as he and his henchman started up after them.

This made the children run all the faster. As they came to the promenade deck and raced beside the railing, a sickening thought hit Pete. What if Seeber were in league with the poachers! Could the riverboat be the hideout for the whole gang?

When the pursuers dropped behind, the fleeing youngsters ducked into a heavily draped salon, then up another flight of stairs. Before them was the wheelhouse. In it was Seeber. He turned around and the youngsters nearly ran straight into his arms.

"Save us!" Pam shouted.

"Here now, calm down," Seeber said with a half smile. "What's going on? And how did you get in here?"

Without naming their pursuers, Pete blurted out

the story. Seeber's face darkened. "Where are those men?" he said. "I'll get them!"

With amazing alacrity for his pudginess, the assistant caretaker bounced down the stairs, hurried through the salon and onto the promenade deck, where he spied the two men. "Get away from here!" he growled. "This is private property."

"Don't let them go!" Pete exclaimed. "We must catch them! They're poachers!"

But Ham Cedars and his companion had turned tail. They ran to the first floor, dashed through the door, around the side of the riverboat, then out the gate, leaving it open.

Pete, Pam, Larry, and Seeber raced behind them. "Come back here, you villains!" the plump man called out, shaking his fist.

The two men hurried into a thicket near the water's edge and popped out, dragging a propeller-driven air boat. They launched it, started the motor, and sped off.

"They're heading around the island," Pam said, stopping short on the beach.

Seeber guessed that they would escape through the channel between Captive Island and the mainland. "They'll probably head south into the Everglades," he said.

The caretaker invited the children to return to the riverboat. "I'll take you on a guided tour," he said, smiling. "You deserve it after that scare."

As they walked through the wire gate again, Pam

wondered why the poachers had been prowling around there.

"Probably to steal canned goods and other supplies to carry back to their hideout," Seeber replied.

Leading the way, the caretaker escorted Pete, Pam, and Larry through the luxurious Mississippi riverboat.

First, they went to a room which housed machinery for turning the paddle wheel. It smelled of grease and iron, and the boys gazed in awe at the huge wheels and gears.

"Okay fellows, let's get on," Seeber said, and walked to a stair leading to the upper part of the boat.

On the next deck there seemed to be no end to the salons, halls, and small parlors. "How beautiful," Pam remarked. "The furnishings are just like in the olden days."

Along the way they came to one door which was locked. "What's in there?" Larry asked.

"I don't know. It's always locked." Seeber replied.

"Supplies or something, I guess." He brushed the question off lightly.

When they reached the top deck, the youngsters looked out over the flat green island. Fluffy white clouds billowed in the blue sky. There was not a boat to be seen.

"Too bad they made their getaway," Pete declared.

"But maybe Dad and Charlie captured them," Pam said hopefully.

Seeber shrugged. "Dragg is pretty slippery," he said and stopped abruptly as Pam wheeled about to face him.

"Is he the blond man?" Her question seemed to take Seeber by surprise.

"Why-ah-er-ah I thought you knew both those men."

"Just by sight," Pete said. Suspicion of Seeber hit him again as they stepped into a large room, heavily draped in red plush.

"I've heard about the gang," the man said calmly. "Read about them in the Fort Myers newspaper. I assumed that the big fellow was Ham Cedars and the other one was Omar Dragg."

Pete and Pam were relieved at the innocent explanation. "We haven't seen a newspaper in some time," Pete said, gazing about the beautiful salon. "How did you get yours?"

Seeber replied that Mr. Dodd had brought one from the mainland on his last trip.

"This must have been the concert room," Pam said, admiring an enormous piano at the far end. "Can't you just see the gentlemen in frock coats and the ladies in all their ruffles and feathers?"

As the children examined the ornate furnishings, their guide excused himself. "I have something I have to attend to in the wheelhouse," he said. "I'll be back in a few minutes."

Having circled the room, Pam stopped beside a heavy satin drapery cord near the doorway. "I wonder what this is for." The two boys walked over to look at it.

"I dare you to pull it," Larry said, grinning.

"It's probably a bell which was used to ring for the servants," Pam guessed.

"Go ahead, tug it," Pete teased.

Pam's eyes danced with delight as she put her hand on the thick cord. "There," she said, jerking it.

Instantly a small square rug on which Pete stood, tilted downward.

"A trap door!" Pam exclaimed as her brother cried out and started to slide through the opening in the floor. Larry grabbed him, and Pete caught hold of the edge of the hole. With Pam and Larry's help he hauled himself to safety.

From his hands and knees, Pete peered into the blackness below. The door, however, suddenly sprang back in place and the small rug looked as if it had not been disturbed at all.

"I wonder if Mr. Seeber knows about this," Larry said.

Pete surmised that no one, other than the owner, knew about the secret trap door.

"Don't you think we should tell someone?" Pam wondered anxiously.

Pete said that he would like to look down into the

Pam jerked the cord.

black hole once again. "It might lead to a dungeon," the boy conjectured.

"But what if you found some skeletons there," Larry put in with a shudder.

Pam was about to pull the rope again when Pete said, "Shh! Listen!"

They heard heavy footsteps hurrying up the stairs below.

Instantly the youngsters froze with fright. Had Cedars and Dragg returned to capture them?

"Quick, hide!" Pete commanded. "Behind the draperies!"

The three covered themselves, making sure that their feet did not stick out below the hem of the heavy, plush curtains. Then they heard muffled voices.

"Don't make a sound," Pete whispered into Pam's ear.

CHAPTER 17

THE STOWAWAY

STANDING like statues, the three children listened to the approaching footsteps.

Suddenly a woman's voice called, "Pete! Pam! Are you in here?"

"Mother!" Pam cried out, as she threw the curtain aside.

"Crickets, Dad!" Pete said. "How did you know where we were?"

"We thought the poachers had come back to get us," Larry spoke up.

Noticing the surprised look on her father's face, Pam told most of what had happened. Just as she reached the part about the trap door, Seeber joined them, and she decided to keep silent about that episode until later.

"This is the man who saved us," Pete said. The introductions were made and Seeber shook hands with Mr. Hollister.

"Nice children you have here," the plump man remarked. "A mite curious, of course. But then we were all young once." He chuckled until his jowls quivered.

As Pete watched, he felt more confused than ever about the assistant caretaker. Was he really sincere, the boy wondered, or only putting on an act for their parents?

By the time Seeber had politely escorted them through the wire gate, Pam's curiosity could contain itself no longer. "Mother, Dad," she asked, "what made you come for us?"

Their father told them that he and Charlie Tiger Tail had been cruising down the shoreline on the way back to camp when they had seen Ham Cedars and Dragg whizzing around Captive Island in an air boat. But by the time Charlie's jet craft had followed them into the channel between there and Turtle Point, the poachers were out of sight. "They certainly disappeared fast," Mr. Hollister added.

"Then Daddy and Charlie cruised around this island where they saw the girls, Ricky, and me collecting shells," Mrs. Hollister put in. "I told them you'd gone to Larry's."

"And after seeing those two men, we were afraid you might be in some kind of danger," Mr. Hollister said, as they walked along the sand, "so we came looking for you. Since there was nobody at Larry's cabin, we guessed you'd gone to the riverboat."

"When we found the open gate and saw footprints, we knew you must be inside," their mother concluded.

After a five-minute walk they came to the place where Charlie and his jet boat awaited them on the beach front. In it were Sue, Holly, and Ricky, along with a collection of the most beautiful shells that Pam had yet seen.

Larry said good-by then and hurried home. It took two trips for the Indian to transport everyone back to the chickee at Turtle Point.

After dinner that evening, when they all sat around the campfire, Pete told about the mysterious trap door.

"Yikes!" Ricky said. "I'd give all my good shells to know what's down there."

"Perhaps it was a hiding place for especially valuable cargo," Mrs. Hollister ventured.

"And maybe someone's hidden in it *right now!*" Holly declared.

"I want to see it," Sue murmured, rubbing her eyes sleepily.

"Daddy," Pam said, "it may sound silly to you, but I don't think the poachers are hiding in the Everglades at all."

In the flickering firelight, everyone looked startled at the girl's remark.

"And where do you think they are?" Pete asked.

"Somewhere on Captive Island," his sister replied. "It was near there that their boat disappeared this afternoon."

Charlie Tiger Tail thought that Pam's hunch was a good one. The men could have slippped ashore unseen from the channel. The side of Captive Island facing the mainland was not only heavily wooded, but deserted.

"No one ever goes there because of the poisonous manchineel trees," he explained, "but experienced Everglades campers could easily avoid them. By the way," he added, "did I ever tell you about the shell mounds on the island?"

"No. What are they?" Holly chirped.

"The prehistoric Indians who lived there ate shellfish," the Seminole said, "and left great piles of shells which have lasted all these years."

"I'd love to see the mounds," Pam said.

"I think we'd better explore all of Captive Island," Pete declared.

Although Charlie Tiger Tail thought that there were no caves where the poachers could hide, he agreed it would be worth searching the next day.

Twice during the night the campers were awakened by the mysterious howling sound. The second time Ricky found it hard to fall asleep again. He tossed and turned on his cot until nearly daybreak.

Just as the sky began to lighten, he slipped quietly from his bed and dressed. By accident he touched Holly's cot and she woke up.

"Where are you going?" she whispered.

"I can't sleep," her brother replied softly. "I'm going down on the beach to look for more shells."

"I'll go with you," Holly said. When she had dressed, the children tiptoed quietly from the chickee and headed for the beach near the cove where the air boats were moored.

The fresh salt breeze whipped through their hair as they scampered along the shore in the dim morning light.

Ricky was stuffing his pockets full of shells when suddenly he pointed to a canoe quietly making its way around Turtle Point. He and Holly ducked into the bushes and watched it for a few moments.

"There're three men in it!" Ricky said.

"Let's run back and tell Daddy!" Holly urged.

"You go," her brother replied. "I'll hide in one of the air boats and spy on those fellows."

As Holly quietly bounded off, Ricky ran for the cove. He reached the propeller air boat, removed a tarpaulin which covered the motor, threw it into the bottom of the craft and hid beneath it. Only his eyes were raised to the level of the gunwales as he watched the canoe.

It came closer and closer.

"Oh, I wish Holly would hurry!" the boy thought to himself, as three men leaped onto the shore and headed straight for the air boat!

Ricky ducked down and hid his head. Then he heard voices.

"We'll steal both boats," one said.

"Do you know how to start the jet?" came another.

This was followed by raucous laughter and a third man said, "Pigeon can start anything."

"Let's run back and tell Daddy!" Holly urged.

Ricky heard their footsteps. Immediately the boat in which he was hiding rocked as someone stepped into it and climbed into the driver's seat.

"Come on, Pigeon, get that jet started," said the man in Ricky's boat.

"All right, all right, Ham," came the reply. "Give me a little time."

"We can't wait forever! It's getting light. They'll be on to us."

Ricky's heart pounded. He heard the muffled sound of tinkering, followed by angry words.

"I hear someone coming!" Ham cried out. "Dragg, Pigeon, come on! We'll take this one!"

"But first we'll upset the jet boat," came Dragg's voice.

Ricky waited tensely, hoping help would arrive in time. Then he heard a loud splash. A moment later the propeller boat rocked violently as the two men jumped in. The motor started with a bang and Ricky could feel the craft lurch forward and skim over the water.

"Oh Daddy, please save me," he thought, as the stolen boat raced over the Gulf waters.

CHAPTER 18

A WHIRLWIND CLIMAX

ON THE SHORE Pete, his father, and Charlie had dressed swiftly and were racing to the cove.

"There they go!" Pete cried. As he pointed to the speeding boat, Mrs. Hollister and the girls came running up behind him.

"They're heading toward Captive Island," Holly said. "Ricky! Where *are* you?"

Mr. and Mrs. Hollister joined in calling to their missing son. When he did not reply, Holly burst into tears.

"He's been kidnaped!" Pam cried out. "Hurry! We must save him!"

The two men, with Pete's help, stepped into the water and righted the overturned jet boat.

"I can't see any damage," Charlie said. He started the engine, and the hot exhaust flattened out the palmetto leaves near the water's edge.

"We have to act fast!" Mr. Hollister said, jumping aboard. He directed his wife to take Holly and Sue in Charlie's truck and drive to the nearest telephone.

"Call the sheriff," he commanded.

"And the junior deputy sheriffs, too," Pete said, as he and Pam hopped in beside their father. "They could all come here in their bus and help us search Captive Island!"

"Great idea," Charlie agreed.

Taking Holly and Sue, Mrs. Hollister hurried off to do her part, and the jet boat roared over the water in pursuit of the fugitives.

By the time Charlie guided his craft into the channel between the mainland and Captive, the sun had come over the horizon and the day was already hot. Even in the clear morning light the searchers could see nothing on the island shore except dense dark vegetation.

Charlie skimmed around the north end of Captive, then back along the Gulf side past the riverboat.

"Look!" Pam cried over the roar of the jet craft. "Mr. Seeber's up in the wheelhouse." As she waved to the man, he ducked out of sight. "That's funny," Pam said. "Why should he hide from us?"

"He's up to something, Dad," shouted Pete. "Maybe he knows where the poachers are."

"Head for shore," Mr. Hollister called to the Indian, "and we'll question him."

"Maybe those men are in there with Ricky!" Pam cried. "Oh, hurry, Charlie!"

The Seminole steered toward land at high speed, but as they neared the beach, a half-submerged log loomed before them. The boat hit it with a hard thud and all four passengers were thrown into the water!

Pam bobbed to the surface, choking from the water she had swallowed. Pete, her father, and Charlie were swimming near her, all headed for the shore.

But the air boat was whizzing around in a great circle.

"Duck!" Mr. Hollister called, as it flashed past them to the beach. There it stopped.

The swimmers staggered onto the sand, shaken but unhurt. They halted instantly at the sound of a mysterious noise which filled the air, louder than they had ever heard it before.

When it died away Pam exclaimed, "That came from the riverboat!"

"Come on," Pete said. "Let's get to the bottom of this!" They raced across the beach and tried the wire gate. It was locked.

"Up and over!" Mr. Hollister commanded. The four scaled the fence and dropped down to the other side. Running ahead, Pete found the door to the steamboat unlocked.

Silently they entered and stood listening in the lobby. There was not a sound. Pete led the way lightly up the spiral stair to the next deck. It was deserted.

Softly they walked along, peeking into rooms, but all were empty. As they approached the one which Mr. Seeber had told them was always locked, Pam clutched her father's sleeve and pointed. The door was ajar!

Mr. Hollister gestured the children to stand back. Warily he pushed the door open, revealing a dim little parlor. Against the back wall stood an old organ and seated before it was Seeber.

"Where's my brother?" Pete cried out.

With a gasp of fright, the fat man whirled, lost his balance and fell backward into the keyboard. As a deafening sound of weird chords filled the room, Mr. Hollister seized the man and pulled him to his feet. "Answer me! Where's my son?"

"And the poachers?" Charlie snapped.

"I—I don't know!"

"You know very well!" declared Pete.

"We're going to search this boat," Charlie said grimly, "and you're coming along."

"Sure, sure!" Seeber agreed docilely.

"We'd better start with the music room," said Pete and led the way up the stairs. As they all entered the spacious parlor, Mr. Hollister and Charlie paused directly over the trap door.

Out of the corner of his eye Pete saw Seeber reach for the drapery cord. "Jump, Dad!" he shouted.

The two men leaped nimbly aside, and in a flash the Indian had Seeber in an iron grip. Pete, meanwhile, grabbed a chair and thrust it into the hole to keep it open.

Pete, Pam, and their father peered down into the darkness. "Ricky!" they called.

"Answer me, son!" Mr. Hollister shouted. There was a faint moan.

"We need a light and a ladder, Seeber," Mr. Hollister said sharply. "Where are they?"

The fat man hung his head. "In the wheelhouse."

Pete and Pam raced away and soon returned with a powerful flashlight and metal folding ladder.

Pam beamed the light onto a figure in the blackness. "Oh!" she exclaimed, "that's not Ricky!" On a cot lay a thin old man. He raised his hand to shield his eyes from the light.

"Help—" the man called out in a tremulous voice.

"It's Mr. Dodd, I'll bet," Pete said.

"Is it?" Charlie asked Seeber.

"Yes, but it's not my fault that he's here. That was Ham Cedars' idea."

Charlie climbed down and returned with Mr. Dodd on his back. He placed the old fellow gently on a sofa.

Mr. Hollister faced Seeber again. "Now where's my son Ricky?"

"I don't know."

"Is this the poacher's hideout?" Pete demanded.

"Not now," Seeber replied. He explained that when Ham Cedars had heard about the riverboat he planned to use it for his headquarters. The gang leader and Seeber had come up the coast to Captive Island and imprisoned Dodd.

"Then we sent Dragg and Pigeon a map with an X marking this place," Seeber said, "and they joined us here. It was bad luck that they lost the map when they chopped down the chickees."

"Who hit the poor crocodile and stole her eggs?" asked Pam.

"And hung up our boat?" added Pete.

"The others did everything," Seeber replied in a wheedling voice. "I was only the lookout. My job was to warn them by sounding the old organ when I saw somebody around. I rigged up an amplifying system so you could hear it for miles. We thought it would scare people away from the island, too. It worked fine until you Hollisters came. You got so nosy that Ham had to move to the cave."

"What cave?" shot Pete.

The fat man bit his lip. "I can't tell you. They'd throw me to the alligators."

Mr. Hollister cut off part of the drapery cord with his pocketknife and tied Seeber's hands behind him. "You come with us," he ordered. "We'll find Ricky!"

"What about Mr. Dodd?" asked Pam.

The real caretaker's eyes were open now and he spoke up in a stronger voice. "Just leave me here and send LeBuff or Larry over to help me. I'll be all right."

Then Seeber was marched to the wire fence. There Charlie took a key from him and opened the

176

gate. In a few minutes the air boat had been pushed into the water and all were aboard. To Charlie's relief the craft started and in a short time he had brought it to shore near Larry's cabin.

Pete raced for the house. Before long he was back with Larry. "Dad will go right over to take care of Mr. Dodd," the island boy assured them.

"Larry can help us look for the cave," Pete put in, as the two boys climbed aboard.

"Seeber," said Charlie angrily, "you tell us where that hideout is right now!" But the fat man seemed too frightened to say anything.

"I don't know of any caves on Captive," Larry spoke up, "and I've explored it all except the shore facing the mainland. That's where the manchineels are."

"Then we'd better search there," said Pam.

Mr. Hollister decided that they should return first to notify his wife, so that she could tell the sheriff where to find them.

Charlie sped for the cove where he moored the jet boat. They all jumped out, and the men hustled Seeber toward the chickee.

As they entered the clearing, Pam gasped in amazement. The big yellow bus stood there, and swarming about it were several dozen junior deputy sheriffs.

"Look, Daddy!" Holly cried out. "We have help."

The sheriff himself was in charge. He was a tall

sun-tanned man with sharp blue eyes. In a twinkling he had signaled one of his two deputies to take care of the fat prisoner.

"You came just in time," Mr. Hollister said. "We have to make a thorough search of Captive Island."

Using the jet craft, one of the sheriff's men began ferrying the junior deputies to the island. Meanwhile, the Hollisters, Larry, and Charlie quickly ate their delayed breakfast while reporting what had happened. Leaving Sue and her mother behind, they joined the assembled searchers on Captive. Then the deputy took off in the air boat to patrol the channel.

"All right, boys," the sheriff boomed, "we'll work our way along the shoreline. If you find anything, whistle. You all know what manchineel trees look like," he added. "Don't go near them."

The young deputies in their white shirts pushed through the scrubby thicket, searching for a cave entrance.

Pete and Pam were in the lead with Holly and Larry close behind. Suddenly Pam stopped. "Wait, listen!" she said.

"Did you hear something?" her brother asked.

"A cry. It sounded like Ricky's."

"Where?"

"Over there," Pam said, pointing to a large hill near the water's edge. It was only six feet high, but very big around and overgrown with vegetation.

"That's a shell mound," said Larry. Pete gave a

low clear whistle. The men and boys came running. At Pete's direction the young deputies cautiously surrounded the mound. They all stopped to listen again. Not a sound, except the distant roar of the jet boat as it guarded the shore.

Pete climbed to the moss-covered top of the hill. Suddenly he motioned back to his father and Charlie. They scrambled up to his side.

"The tarpaulin from our boat!" Pete said. It lay flat on the top of the mound as if covering something.

Mr. Hollister motioned to the sheriff to quiet the young deputies. Then he reached down and whipped the canvas aside.

Beneath it was a gaping hole!

"The entrance to the cave," Pete cried out.

As he did, a man's head appeared. His huge hands gripped the side of the opening and he pulled himself out.

"That's Ham Cedars!" Pam shouted from below. "Catch him!" But before the words were out of her mouth, Mr. Hollister and Charlie had tackled the fellow and all three rolled over and over down the side of the shell mound.

At a cry from the sheriff, the deputies swarmed up the sides of the mound. When Omar Dragg struggled to come up out of the hole, he was caught by a dozen young arms and hustled down to the sheriff.

The man called Pigeon was next. He had even

Beneath it was a gaping hole!

less of a chance! And following abjectly were the two poachers who had snatched the spear from Pete. After the prisoners had been handcuffed, Pete, Pam, Holly, Mr. Hollister, and Charlie descended rough steps cut into the interior of the shell mound.

At the bottom, the hollowed-out hill opened into a large cavern. It was dimly lit by sunlight which filtered through crevices in the rock ceiling.

There in a corner lay Ricky, bound and gagged. Pete ran to free him.

"Oh Daddy, am I glad to see you!" Ricky cried, as his father hugged him.

"Tell us what happened!" said Pete.

"Well," replied Ricky, "you should have seen me underneath that tarpaulin in the boat! Yikes, I was almost afraid to breathe! Finally the boat slowed down and stopped. I felt the poachers get out, and I thought I'd escape as soon as they went away. But just then I heard one of them say, 'Wait a minute. We need a cover over the hole on top of the mound. Let's take this tarpaulin.' Then he yanked it away and there I was!"

"Oh," gasped Holly. "What did you do?"

"I tried to run, but they grabbed me, and tied me up. At first I couldn't figure out where I was, but I heard them say we were in the shell mound."

"You mean the boat came right in here?" Charlie asked in surprise.

"That's right," said Ricky. "There's a passage cut into the mound from the water. We couldn't see it because it's all covered with hanging moss. I'll show you."

Ricky led his father out of the cavern and across the shell mound to the stolen air boat and the poachers' craft. Everyone followed.

Without delay the boats were floated from the mound hideout and the poachers were herded into one of them.

As the prisoners were ferried across the channel to Turtle Point, the junior deputies let out a wild victory cry.

"Hurray for Pete and Ricky!" yelled Alf Cohen.

"Hurray for Pam too!" said Bud Lardner. "I think we ought to make her an honorary member."

"Let's take a vote right now," said Wyn Gillis. "All in favor say 'aye.'"

A great cheer rose, and the "ayes" could be heard all the way to the chickee at Turtle Point. Pam blushed at the honor.

After the bus had left with the deputies and their prisoners, the Hollisters, Charlie, and Larry spent their last evening together around a glowing campfire. As the sun set, the island boy slipped off to get more wood, and moments later raced into sight.

"Come on," he called. "The biggest sea turtle I've ever seen is on the beach!"

Pete swung Sue onto his back and the five Happy Hollisters ran toward the shore. There, a huge turtle was waddling toward the surf. It stopped and swung its head from side to side.

"Yikes, that's the greatest!" Ricky exclaimed, and turned cart wheels on the sand.

Sue wriggled from Pete's back like a little bug. Before he could stop her, she had run to the turtle and climbed onto its shell.

"Sue, come here!" Pam called out in alarm.

The turtle paid no attention to its passenger, but began to move again toward the water. Holly dashed in front of the sea creature, waving her arms to stop it.

As the youngsters gasped, Sue held onto the slippery seat for a few moments, then tumbled onto the sand and laughed. Holly nimbly jumped aside. The turtle bobbed its head, and with a splash flopped into the Gulf of Mexico.